THE

HUMAN

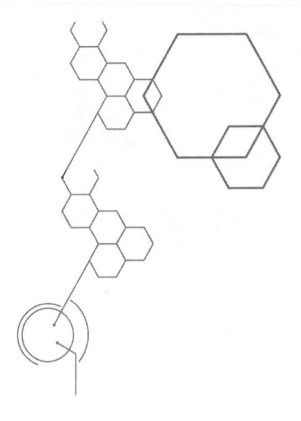

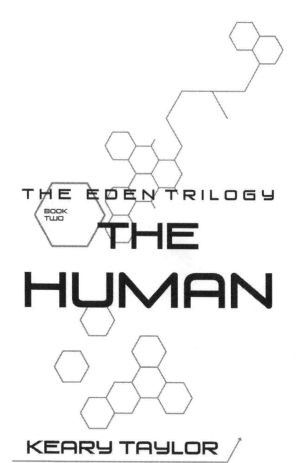

THE EDEN TRILOGY

BOOK TWO

THE HUMAN

KEARY TAYLOR

First Print Edition: June 2013

Cover Design by Keary Taylor
Cover Image: Shutterstock.com

Taylor, Keary, 1987-
The Human : a novel / by Keary Taylor. – 1st ed.

ISBN: 978-0615827704

KEARY
TAYLOR
BOOKS

ALSO BY KEARY TAYLOR

ONE

Nearly everywhere I looked, there were bodies.

They lay limp in the streets. They were piled on top of each other inside buildings. They sat still and slumped over inside vehicles.

We were surrounded by over three million decomposing, cybernetic-infused corpses.

I closed my eyes as a sense of overwhelming vertigo seized me. Rubble fell from the roof, down into the street below, as I took one step back from the ledge.

There were so many bodies. They surrounded us on all sides. Silent and immobile. They were dead. They couldn't infect us anymore.

But I had lived my whole life running from them.

Every instinct in me wanted to flee the city.

I opened my eyes, turning them east. I missed the mountains. I missed the trees. I missed the heat and the snow and the changing leaves.

I missed protecting my family. I missed staying up all night to make sure we were safe.

I missed having a purpose.

1

We were safe now. The Bane in the city were destroyed.

What purpose did I serve now?

I took two more steps back, bumping into the Pulse. Its sharp edges dug into my ribs, but I stayed pressed into it, hoping to feel something other than guilt and loss.

I'd had a purpose then. I'd helped to clear this city. So had many others.

But not all of us had made it out.

And my actions ate at me every day.

"Eve?"

Avian stepped out onto the roof of the hospital. A rifle was slung over his shoulder, a utility belt hanging low on his narrow hips. His eyes were serious and searching as he met mine.

I looked back out over the city to the east. His footsteps approached, slow but knowing.

He stepped in front of me, locking his eyes on mine. He placed a hand on either side of my face and pressed his forehead to mine.

"We can leave," he breathed as my eyes slid closed. "You don't have to stay here and torture yourself."

I shook my head slightly and the air around me seemed to tighten and constrict around my chest and throat.

"I can't abandon them," I whispered, placing my hand on Avian's chest. The only sure thing in my world, Avian's heart beat back the echo of everything I had ever fought for. "I have to deal with the messes I've made."

"You've saved them, Eve," he said. His rough cheek brushed mine as his lips whispered next to my ear. "Maybe it's time to save yourself."

I didn't respond because I would never be able to make him understand the weight and turmoil that burned through my veins. I simply pressed my face into Avian's neck and crushed him into my chest.

"Come on," Avian said after a long while, taking my hand. He pulled me toward the stairs that led back into the hospital. "Dinner will be ready soon."

We made our way to the armory, finding it empty.

We didn't really need weapons anymore, but not a single one of our scouts was going to walk around the city without a firearm.

Instincts don't die quickly.

A rack of firearms lined one wall. There were labels below each shotgun or rifle. I had six firearms myself. Avian had five. And those were just the ones we kept in the armory.

My eyes hesitated on one name.

West.

His rifle and shotgun had sat untouched for weeks.

Static crackled over my radio, making me jump.

"It's happening again! I need you up here, Eve! Now!"

Royce. There was unmistakable frustration and fear in his voice.

My teeth threatened to break as my jaw clenched. I placed my M4 assault rifle back on the rack and looked over at Avian. He hesitated for a moment, the pain of the past

3

surfacing once more like a heavy, dark cloud. He finally gave an assuring nod.

"I'm on my way," I said into the radio. I squeezed Avian's shoulder, hoping it was reassuring. "I'll be back as soon as I can."

"Yeah," was all he said. The muscles in his neck tightened and his eyes darted away from mine. He went back to cleaning his weapon.

My footsteps echoed off the walls. The hospital felt so quiet and yet so busy these days. In the two months since the Pulse went off, everyone had slowly started moving out. But the hospital remained the base of operations here in Los Angeles, now renamed New Eden. It was still the most secure location and all of our military supplies, food, and medical equipment remained stored within its walls.

I jogged up six flights of stairs and exited onto the blue floor.

"Eve!" I heard Royce bellow from down the hall. "Take your time. It's not like he isn't trying his best to kill us!"

I picked up my pace, sprinting toward the door I was becoming all too familiar with.

"For a robotic freak you sure can be slow," Royce growled as he helped Graye hold the door shut. Something slammed against it from the other side. They groaned as their feet slid back and the door jerked open a few inches.

"How long ago did he wake up?" I asked, pressing my palm flat against the door, pushing it back shut. I avoided looking thorough the tiny window made of reinforced glass.

"It's been about twenty minutes," Graye answered. "He was pretty out of it for a bit, then he freaked out."

4

I nodded, feeling everything in me tire. This whole process exhausted me mentally and physically, and it just kept repeating.

"I've got it," I said. "You two can leave now."

"You sure you can handle him?" Royce asked. "He's raging today."

I wasn't ready, at all. But I wouldn't tell Royce that. "Yeah."

Finally he nodded.

"Count of three?" I asked. "One, two, three!"

They jumped away as I yanked the door open, stepped inside, and slammed the door closed behind me. I broke the door handle off, locking the both of us inside until I could get him to cooperate and help me force it open.

I heard him freeze behind me.

It took a long time to turn away from the door. The last seven weeks had been painful. I'd been preparing myself for a bad situation, because there was no easy way for this all to end. But I hadn't expected this to end like it did.

"Eve," he breathed behind me. I heard him take a step closer and everything in me wanted to retreat, to not have to go through all of this, again and again. "What's going on?"

Collecting myself, I turned, and looked at West.

He wasn't as bad as Elijah. He'd at least kept both his eyes. But the skin was bubbled on the right side of his face, the left had a few scattered scars. His face was in bad shape, there was no question about it. His entire body was covered in marks and scar tissue. I could barely distinguish the claw marks on his neck—which had once been so prominent— from the new scars.

He was broken, but he was still West.

Even if he wasn't my West.

Even if he couldn't remember that.

"What happened to me?" he asked for the third time. "What is this?"

My eyes dropped to his bare chest. A device was implanted there, just above his heart, and small barbs disappeared into his skin. Components swirled, ticked, and spun, casting a pale green glow, keeping it charged at all times.

Keeping me away at all times.

"It's keeping you human," I said with a hard swallow. I didn't know how many times I could keep doing this.

West stared at me for a long time, like he couldn't quite make sense of my words. He looked back down at the device, his fingers touching where it went into his bare chest.

"I..." he stuttered. "I remember... I remember going to the plant, all the Bane. I was helping Royce repair the line. A gun fired... I don't remember how I got back here."

I recalled the night I had been at the power plant myself. My mission had been to connect the power line for the Pulse to the power source. There had been hundreds of Bane gathered around it. There were flashes of light, gunfire, explosions. I'd nearly lost my legs that night. But it had been for nothing.

The Bane had pulled the line, and West went with a team to try and fix it.

I shifted from one foot to the other, again fighting the urge to run. I was having a hard time meeting his eyes.

"You were attacked," I explained. "The Bane got you. You were infected."

"Infected?" he said, his voice breathy with shock and disbelief. "No, I couldn't... I can't... I made it this long!"

"I know," I said, debating if I could walk away from the door or not. West was unpredictable when he forgot. He had a tendency to break things—and sometimes people.

I finally stepped away from the door and crossed to the small metal chair in the corner, opposite of where West stood. On the nightstand next to me, West's grandfather's notebook rested so innocently on it.

"The night you all fixed the power supply to the Pulse, you were infected. No one saw the Bane that was hiding. Royce and his men got you back here and put you under the Extractor. We weren't sure if you were going to make it or not. No one was sure how long it had been since you were touched."

"Royce said it had to be under an hour," West said. He rubbed the device in his chest absent mindedly. "That was the magic number."

I nodded. I pressed my palms flat against each other between my knees, rubbing them together slowly. "We watched you for a long time, waiting to see if we could get all the cybernetics out. Normally the process takes about ten days. We waited fifteen."

I'd fought Royce the final three days. He wanted to dispose of West, certain it had been too late to save him. The only living TorBane in the city was trapped in West's body and Royce wasn't willing to risk the safety of our people over one man.

In the end, Royce gave West a few more days. West had woken up just in time.

"So they fixed me, right?" West said, his voice full of hope and fear at the same time. "I mean, I'm alive. I don't feel like infecting everyone, so that means it worked?"

I tried to nod, to reassure him that he was going to be okay. But that glowing inhibitor was right there in front of me.

"Not exactly," I said, my palms turning white as I pressed them together harder. "They thought they had everything out. But Dr. Beeson did a scan, and saw one small piece left. A half inch long, an eighth of an inch wide. That's all that's left. It's relatively tiny. But it's formed in your heart. They can't get it out, not without killing you."

West stared at me, almost like he hadn't heard me. I wondered for a moment if he was lapsing again.

"And this?" he finally said, so quiet, even I almost didn't hear him. Then he glanced down at the device.

"Like I said, it's keeping you human," I started explaining. I rubbed a hand over my eyes, just wanting to skip the rest of this day and go home to bed. "That scrap inside of you is still TorBane. It still wants to spread throughout your body. That inhibitor is keeping it from spreading. Well, slowing it down."

"Slowing it down?" West asked as he sank onto his bed. "Not fully stopping it?"

I shook my head. "It keeps it at bay for about two weeks at a time, but no. It doesn't stop it permanently. You have to go back in the Extractor every two weeks."

West stared at me in disbelief for a moment. "How do you know all this? How... How long has this been going on?"

"Just short of two months," I answered him hollowly. I sat back in the chair, my arms crossing over my chest. "You've undergone extraction three times now. And every time you come back out, you don't remember what's happened."

West shook his head, squeezing his eyes closed tightly, like maybe he could shake the memories into focus.

"You should probably get some rest, eat some food," I said, climbing to my feet. "I will walk with you to the kitchen, let them know you're okay."

"Did I hurt anyone?" he asked. "They've got me locked up. There must be a reason for that."

I stilled by the door. The first time he had woken, Dr. Beeson had been there, as well as some of his team. He had broken three of Dr. Beeson's fingers and the arm of his assistant, Addie. "It doesn't matter," I said after too long of a pause. "We just need to focus on getting you better."

West turned toward the mirror that hung on the wall. Or what remained of it. He had thrown a book at it the second time he woke up and broken it pretty badly. His face paled when he saw his reflection. One of his hands rose to touch his skin.

"Come on," I said uncomfortably, trying to draw his attention away from what he was seeing. "Let's get you some food."

"I'm not hungry," he said, still studying his reflection.

"Fine," I said. "Help me get the door open?"

9

West didn't respond. His head whipped to the right, toward the small window that looked out to the sunny street below. He crossed to it, looking out.

"It worked?" he breathed. "Didn't it?"

I nodded, even though he wasn't looking at me. "Yeah, the Pulse killed them all off. We're safe, for now."

West took a deep breath and continued to stare out the window for a long moment. "I can't believe I missed it."

It was my fault he had. He'd been trying to protect me when he got infected.

Finally, he turned. With his help, we forced the door open. I stepped out into the hall.

"Are you going to terrorize anyone, or do I need to send up an armed guard?" I asked, shoving my hands into my pockets. It might have sounded like I was making a joke, but I wasn't.

"I feel okay. Freaked out, but okay." He shook his head when he looked out into the hall, realizing he was on the blue floor and not the residential second floor.

"Good," I said, turning to go.

I'd only taken two steps away from West when he called out to me.

"You chose Avian, didn't you?"

I hesitated mid-step, a sharp, biting cold spreading through my veins. I had hoped we could avoid this part for just a little while longer this time around.

"Yes," I answered simply. Without waiting for his reply, I kept walking down the hall.

10

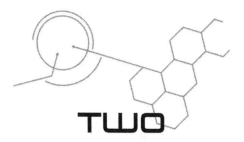

TWO

"Are you okay?"

My eyes jerked to the right, finding Lin walking out of room 104. The room behind her was filled with children. They sat in a circle, reading books and coloring pictures. Lin was the new-age elementary school teacher.

I'd been standing in the lobby, zoned out, trying not to think about West or cybernetics or Bane or the complexity of love. She stopped at my side, her arms folded across her tiny frame. "West woke up, didn't he?" she asked.

I nodded, pressing my lips tightly together. My eyes searched the lobby.

"I think Avian went back to his room," Lin said as she too scanned the space. It wasn't as busy as it had been a few weeks ago. The day-to-day operations of New Eden had changed. We didn't have to worry about the Bane falling down on us. For now.

"West was pretty calm this time," I said, looking back toward the classroom. Parents came to collect their children. Wix took Brady by the hand and led him out into the sun outside. "Once I got there anyway."

11

"Are *you* okay though?" Lin asked. Her eyes searched for the truth I knew she'd find.

My eyes rose to the ceiling and I shook my head. "I don't know," I said quietly. "He asked about my decision almost immediately."

"It's still fresh for him," Lin said.

"It's always fresh for him," I said, wrapping my arms around my midsection. "That's the problem. I keep trying to move on, to let go of the guilt I feel. But him forgetting every time makes that impossible."

"You don't need to punish yourself," Lin said, placing a tiny hand on my arm. "You deserve to be happy, Eve. You can't save everyone and you can't always fix every problem."

I met her gaze again and I felt an immense sense of gratitude toward her. Lin was one of the most understanding people I had ever met. I couldn't comprehend how she could always take things so calmly and evenly. But she always said the right things when I needed to hear them.

"Thanks," I said, attempting a bit of a smile.

"Any time," she said before wrapping me in a hug that was surprisingly strong, considering her size.

"I think I'm going to go find Avian now," I said when she released me.

"I think that's a good idea," she said with a wink before she walked back to the remaining students.

Climbing the stairs, I turned down the hall. I knocked on Avian's door once. No one answered so I peeked inside, only to find it empty.

I opened the door to my own room to find a small package sitting on my bed. I crossed the room and gingerly picked it up.

It was solid, far heavier than I expected it to be.

Tearing back the brown paper packaging, I found a box. I lifted the lid to find a beautiful, silver handgun.

"I kind of thought it just screamed 'Eve.'"

I turned to see Avian leaning in the doorframe, his arms crossed over his chest.

"Is this a Desert Eagle .44 magnum?" I asked, my voice disbelieving. I looked back at the firearm. I pulled the clip out and found it fully loaded.

"Yep," Avian said, crossing the room and stopping by my side. "I found it while I was out with the rehoming crew."

"These are nearly impossible to find," I said with a laugh in my voice. "And you just happen across one?"

Avian placed his hands on my shoulders. He leaned in close, brushing his lips across my shoulder. "Uh huh."

"You want to go test it out after duty tomorrow?" I asked, replacing the clip and eying along the barrel.

"I was hoping you would say that," he said and I could hear the smile in his voice. "I got myself a new compound bow and a quiver full of broad tipped carbon shaft arrows. I wanted to test them out."

Setting the gun down on the bed, the safety on, I turned and faced Avian. He wrapped his arms around my waist and pulled me in close. There was a hint of a smile playing in the corners of his mouth.

"Are you using firearms to get me alone in my room?" I asked.

"I wouldn't dream of it," he said, his smile growing as he pushed the door closed.

Avian's lips were as familiar as the feeling of clothing against my skin, but he was different fabrics and textures every time they met. His lips consumed my own, trailed to my jaw, explored my neck, sought other places on my body.

I lay back on the bed, my new firearm hard under my spine. Avian lifted me further onto the bed and he shifted on top of me. My hands clutched the fabric of his shirt and as his lips trailed once again to my throat, the fabric suddenly split as I tugged. Neither of us noticed as I let the tattered remains fall to the floor.

Avian was the one sure way to pull me back to the surface on my dark, drowning days.

His hands held the small of my back, his skin meeting mine in a way that threatened to black me out. My breath came out ragged in a way hours of running never managed to bring out of me.

I tugged on his lower lip with my teeth, my hand running over his buzzed hair. I loved it when it got to this length. It was soft and fuzzy. I rolled on top of him, my legs straddling his.

Somehow we'd found heaven on Earth in the middle of hell. Avian and I together, that was what it was. Heaven. Happiness.

There was a knock on the door. "Eve?" Royce's voice rang though the heavy wood. "You in there?"

I jerked back from Avian, covering my mouth to stifle the scream or laugh I knew was about to come. My face felt warm and I knew I was blushing.

"Yeah, I'm here," I said, springing off of Avian and straightening my clothes. I half-tripped across the room and cracked the door open.

Royce shook his head, a coy smile playing on his lips that said he knew exactly what I had just been doing.

"You need something?" I squeaked.

"Dr. Beeson and Dr. Stone would like a report on West," Royce said. His own face was slightly red with embarrassment.

"Okay, I'll be up in a few minutes," I said, my voice higher pitched than I would have liked.

"Five minutes," he said, attempting to be serious once again. "Oh, and Avian," he said loudly. My face flushed all the more hot. "Nice work on the block five scout. Looks like those units will be perfect."

"Thank you, Sir," Avian called from behind me. I faintly heard him suppressing a laugh.

Royce just shook his head as he walked away. I heard him mutter something like "horny hybrid" under his breath.

I turned back to Avian, feeling utterly horrified.

Avian burst into laughter.

"This is not funny, Avian!" I said, throwing a box of tissues in his direction.

He just laughed as he dodged them. "I have to say, I never thought I'd have the experience of being walked in on by the father with you," he said.

"Royce…" I started to argue.

"He might as well be," Avian said, the smile still on his face. "Trust me, he's protective enough of you to be your father."

My face still felt hot. "Well, I'm fully aware of what the human emotion of embarrassment feels like now."

Avian chuckled and bent to grab his shirt. He held up the tattered remains with a ridiculous smile.

"Sorry about that," I said, not feeling sorry in the slightest.

"Don't worry about it," he said light-heartedly as he dropped it into my garbage can. "I can always get another in this city."

I couldn't help but stare at him for a moment. He really was beautiful. His eyes burned bright in the dim light, his brow heavy and dark, giving him a deep and soulful look. His jaw was strong, all his features so serious and deep. I'd heard stories about angels—beautiful, good, and perfect creatures that came from heaven and walked the earth.

Avian was an angel if ever there were one.

"You'd better get going or you're going to get in trouble with your dad," Avian teased, pressing a kiss to my forehead. I punched him in the arm, maybe a little too hard considering he winced.

"Thank you for the gun," I said, truly meaning it.

"You're welcome," he said, pressing a kiss to my lips.

THREE

That night, Avian had a nightmare about Sarah. They came frequently and ferociously. It was the guilt of leaving her behind, back in the mountains. It ate at him. He knew there had been nothing he could do about it. But that didn't prevent the nightmares.

Nights like those he found his way into my bed.

I woke again sometime around four in the morning. Seeing Avian still asleep, I slid out from next to him, pulled my work clothes and boots on, and slipped out the door. I made my way through the dark halls to the kitchen, my stomach growling. Coming to Los Angeles had been good for everyone in Eden. We had all been starving when we arrived, trying to survive off of dwindling food stores after the Bane burned the gardens to ash.

The kitchen was dark, as it should be this time of night. Everyone was adjusting back to a diurnal sleeping schedule quickly.

Flipping a light on, I went for the refrigerator.

"I take it you couldn't sleep either?"

My fingers flew to the gun at my hip and I poised it in front of me.

"I see all your old habits haven't died just yet," West said, his familiar cocky grin cracking on his lips. His face looked more like its old self when he smiled. He sat on the counter, a half-eaten carrot in one hand. "Still the same old gun-happy Eve."

"Geeze, West," I griped at him, slipping my gun back into its holster. I reached for an orange from the fridge. "Were you trying to get your head shot off?"

"If someone is going to do it, it might as well be you," he said, hopping down from the counter.

"What are you doing up right now?" I asked, digging my fingers into the rind of the orange. Its strong odor flooded my nose.

"Couldn't sleep," he said, leaning back against the upper cabinets. "Nightmares."

I nodded. I knew what that was like. But lately my nightmares usually involved West.

He stood there for a long minute, staring at me as I ate the orange. I couldn't quite meet his eyes. I fought the urge to turn and leave, to not have to answer the million questions and accusations I knew were running through his head.

"You're different," West finally said. My eyes rose to meet his as I wiped my hands on my pants. My heart was beating just a little too fast. He slid off the counter.

West took a step closer to me. I could see the conflict in his face. Before, he would have reached for me, touched my face, tried to take my hand. But I had made my choice. And it wasn't him. "You seem…older? More beaten."

18

"What's that supposed to mean?" I asked, trying to keep my voice hard. I wasn't going to show how uncomfortable I was. I wasn't going to let him get to me.

"Was it easy?" he asked. "Just flipping it off like that?"

"West, don't do this," I said, shaking my head.

"This kind of seems like something we should talk about," he said. There was obvious pain in his eyes. There was anger right alongside it. "Don't you think?"

"We have talked about it," I replied softly, my eyes dropping.

West faltered at that.

We had talked, the first time he had woken up. He'd been in disbelief, over his infection, over my choice, over what he was to do with his future.

"This hasn't been easy for you, has it?" he asked, taking another half step forward. "What happened to me?"

"Doesn't that sound a bit presumptuous to you?" Something stung under the surface of my skin and my eyes dropped to the blue glow of West's inhibitor.

"I know you, Eve," West said, his voice growing quiet. He reached up and pushed a loose strand of hair behind my ear, bringing him even closer. It felt like all my bones were seizing up, my blood hissing to life. "Better than even Avian knows you. You might have picked him, but I know what happened to me had an effect on you."

"Not like you're thinking though," I managed to say. My jaw clenched, pain prickling along my bones. "I couldn't live with the guilt, knowing you didn't know what I had done, that I'd finally made my choice."

19

"Are you sure that's it?" West asked, his finger tracing along my cheek.

My breath caught in my throat. My lungs felt like they were being pulled out through my rib cage. "Unlike you West, I don't keep everything hidden, masking the truth at all times. I picked Avian, end of story."

A painful half smile formed on West's face. He gave the smallest of nods. "Then why doesn't it feel that way?"

My bones were starting to splinter as the device embedded into West pulled at all the cybernetic and mechanical parts inside of me.

"West," I breathed, my voice coming out as a whisper.

"Yes?" he replied hopefully. He came closer, so close our clothes were touching.

"You're hurting me," I forced out, barely able to breathe anymore.

"Trust me," he said, his expression hardening. "It's nothing like how I've been hurting since that night on the transformer."

"No—" I hissed, my eyes squeezing closed.

"She means you're physically ripping her apart," a voice from behind us suddenly said. "You should really step away before you kill her."

I couldn't even turn my head but I knew Royce's voice. West's eyes widened, panic flashing across his face. He scrambled away from me, backing up against the stainless steel counter.

I collapsed to the ground on my hands and knees, my breath coming in and out in painful gulps.

Royce's boots came into view and I felt his calloused hands around my arms, helping me to my feet again.

"I'm sorry," West stammered. "I didn't realize this thing would affect her like that."

"You're an idiot then," Royce said, his voice hard. Sure I would be okay, he turned toward West, his fist balled. "That thing controls what her entire body is made of. You never stopped to consider that?"

My eyes rose to West. He looked tortured, pain at his unknown actions plain on his face. A part of me wanted to feel sorry for him, to tell him it was okay. But forgiving West was something I was getting tired of doing.

"I don't particularly like the fact that the last remaining infected person within one hundred miles is walking around my base, but because of Eve's insistence I've allowed you to stay. Don't give me a reason to get rid of you," Royce's voice dripped with ice. "She's our most valuable asset here in New Eden next to the Pulse. And you…are not."

Royce's hardness was startling and I saw the fear in West's eyes.

"Eve?" another voice said from the entrance to the kitchen. I turned to see Avian looking at us, uncertainty on his face. "What's going on?"

I glanced back toward West, guilt and shame racing through my blood.

Avian looked from West to me and I saw his eyes harden. "Did he hurt you?"

"No, Avian, I'm—" I started to say, but Avian was suddenly across the kitchen, right up in West's face.

"Keep your distance with that thing," Avian said. "Or I swear—"

"Avian!" I yelled, pulling on the back of his shirt. He stumbled back four steps but his gaze remained locked on West. West glowered back.

"Take Eve back to her room," Royce growled, pushing Avian gently back with a hand on his chest. "Make her get some rest."

After a long while, Avian nodded, tearing his eyes from West to look at me. His expression softened only slightly.

I couldn't meet his eyes and I hated that.

The radio crackled later that afternoon. Royce was calling for the weekly meeting.

As people gathered around me in the conference room, I wondered if this was how society worked before—leaders meeting to discuss how things should run and planning how to keep everyone alive.

But before the Evolution they didn't have to rebuild from scratch. They didn't have to talk about where to find food, to scavenge new homes, to have to haul away decomposing bodies.

I sat at the long table, between Avian and Gabriel— Eden's former leadership—joined by half a dozen others, Royce and Elijah included.

"Welcome, everybody," Royce started out as he walked into the room. He pulled his chair back and took a seat. He folded his arms on the table, his grey eyes turning to meet ours. "Bet ten years ago you never thought you'd be on the board of what's left of humanity."

A few people chuckled, but most just gave a tight-lipped smile, not always appreciative of Royce's harsh and blunt humor.

"Let's go over the weekly report," Royce said, pulling out a notepad and a pen. The sight was strange, too relaxed and too organized for our chaotic world. "Tuck, why don't you start us out?"

Tuck cleared his throat as he stood. His eyes shifted just a little too fast from his own notebook to the faces around the table. Tuck had gone from simple watchman in Eden to leader of the Bane Removal Crew, or the BRC, in New Eden.

"We cleared block sixteen this week, and got half of block seventeen cleared," he said as he walked to the map that hung on one of the walls, marking block sixteen with a big red X. "No issues reported." We had created this map with the hospital as ground zero, sectioning off each block spreading out around us. The bodies may have been dead, TorBane destroyed, but no one wanted to see the hundreds of thousands of bodies lying everywhere. And the remaining decomposing human flesh was a health hazard.

"How close are we to filling the first shipper?" Royce asked as he studied the map.

"It's only about half filled," Tuck said. "We've sealed off the filled areas. It should be ready to send out in another three weeks."

I'd seen the huge ships once, docked out at the edge of the ocean. Tuck told me they were called cruise ships and that once upon a time people boarded them for relaxing trips out on the water.

"Great," Royce said, turning his attention to his notebook again, scribbling something down. "The quicker we get those bodies cleared out, the better."

"And the rehoming crew?" Royce asked.

"We've continued with the housing scout," Elijah said. It was always painful to look at him. He was a harsh reminder that West could have turned out so much worse. "Team one cleared block seven yesterday. We should be able to set up three units in it."

"Team two finished up block five, as you know," Avian said. Unlike me, Avian did have a purpose here in New Eden. He and Elijah had their own teams that scouted out new homes for us all to start inhabiting.

I couldn't stand working on the rehoming crew. Finding a new home in the city meant I would be trapped here forever. Thinking about that made me want to do self-destructive things.

But for everyone else, getting a new home outside the hospital meant the return to a more normal life. One that resembled the world before the Evolution.

"I've also been working with them on emergency medical care," Avian said. "Dr. Reziks and Dr. Sun have been assisting me."

Royce nodded as he continued scribbling notes down. "Great. Gabriel, what about your end?"

Gabriel cleared his throat, sitting up a little straighter in his seat. I still couldn't get over how different he looked with his beard neat and trimmed, his hair cut short. He

24

looked like a totally different man. He appeared at least ten years younger.

"We've split civilians into two groups. The first is in charge of food and general goods regulation. There are two subgroups of this one. One half is in charge of the garden and scouring the city for non-perishables. The other half is in charge of setting up a supply store. They are currently developing a regulation system so people can go and get what they need.

"The second group is in charge of cleaning up the units the rehoming scouts deem safe. There was a former general contractor here in Los Angeles as well as an electrician. Together they are heading up a team to start in blocks three and six and make them fit to reside in. We've already established six homes in block four and they are currently being inhabited."

It was strange hearing Gabriel try and succeeding in sounding so official. He was attempting to prove that he was every bit as capable of leading as Royce was. Not that he needed to. Royce might have been a genius when it came to leading the military and scientific side of New Eden, but he was often too brutal and blunt to connect with everyone else. People naturally looked to and trusted Gabriel.

"And how are our survivors adapting?" Royce asked.

"They're… adjusting," Gabriel said. "It hasn't been easy for them, but given what they've gone through, it isn't surprising."

About a week after the second half of Eden arrived in New Eden, Tuck and his then small crew found three people in a building, hiding and terrified. They were young, ages sixteen, seventeen, and nineteen. They'd survived the last five years by holing up in a police station, locking themselves behind bars during the day, boarding up the doors and windows, and only venturing out in the dead of night to find food and supplies. Two of them were siblings, the youngest another girl they had found. They were all half-starved.

And then a few days later a group of four more survivors walked right into the hospital. They'd been watching us for two days, and finally decided we were safe to approach. They'd all been hiding in a similar way the last few years.

In a city that once had a population of nearly four million, there were now only one hundred forty-three known survivors and a quarter of us had immigrated from elsewhere.

"And lastly, Erik," Royce said, pulling me back into the room.

"The radio message is up and running still, broadcasting on a constant loop over five different stations," Dr. Beeson said. "We can't be sure, but we're estimating the signal should be able to be heard and found within a fifteen-hundred-mile radius. If someone turns a radio on and scans, they'll find the message."

I'd been there when Royce recorded that message. The message that said we'd cleared New Eden, that it was safe, that we could provide food and shelter if one could get here. Royce gave our exact location.

So far no one had come.

Considering how the Bane continued to Evolve, how they'd hunted us down, burned our gardens to starve us out, there was probably no one left out there. The Bane were getting too smart and too aggressive.

Yet I felt uneasy about the message. If they looked, anyone could find it. Just because someone was human didn't mean they could be trusted.

"And we're checking incoming signals?" Royce asked.

"All hours of the day," Dr. Beeson said. "Now that they don't have the Pulse to focus on, it's something to keep my team busy."

Royce chuckled, crinkle lines forming around his eyes. "I can only imagine what a team of bored scientists will do to keep themselves entertained." This time most of the room did laugh at Royce's more appropriate joke.

"They're still mourning that they're done with their greatest creation," Dr. Beeson joked. "They're missing their work on the Pulse."

"I still think that once we've gotten everyone settled in their own residences we should rebuild the energy storage devices," I said. I wasn't in charge of anything, the only one in this room without a purpose, but they still allowed me to sit in on these meetings.

"I was just talking to Royce about that this morning," Dr. Beeson said with a nod. "We have no guarantee that the city will stay clear. Once things settle down with the rehoming, my team will be back on it."

I nodded. Avian squeezed my knee under the table. He and I discussed the possibility of the Bane migrating back into the city often.

"Unless you have anything more, Gabriel?" Royce said. Gabriel shook his head. "Then I think that is all for today. We'll meet again same time next week."

FOUR

Dinner consisted of canned chicken, canned green beans, and canned potatoes. I would have fought off ten Bane if it meant I could have gotten my hands on some fresh spinach or wild berries.

When I was finished eating I started down the hall toward the stairs that led up to my room.

I was just about to pass the medical wing when I heard Avian's voice.

"—getting worse," he said, his voice low. "I don't know that it's going to get any better while she stays in the city."

"It certainly sounds like conditional depression." It was Dr. Sun who replied. "Given her history, it is understandable that she would be having a hard time dealing with all of the changes."

"She's worked so hard all her life," Avian mused. "I never thought I'd say something like this, but I think life is too easy here. She doesn't know how to handle it."

"Depression is easy to slip into when you don't have any goals to work toward."

29

Their words stung like a hundred yellow jackets.

Depression. I was depressed?

There wasn't room in this world for depression.

Balling my fists, I continued down the hall and up the stairs to my room.

I closed the door behind me, leaning back on it. I let my eyes fall closed and pressed my hands in on either side of my head.

Goals. What goals had I had before the Pulse went off?

Survive. Protect my family.

What was I working for anymore?

Nothing.

And it was mentally breaking me.

Letting out a slow breath, internally telling myself to calm down, I opened my eyes.

There was a folded piece of paper lying on my bed. I crossed the room and picked it up. The page was half filled with sloppy handwriting.

> *You were obsessed with manuals as a kid. You read faster than anyone I'd ever met and you always wanted to read the most boring stuff. Someone left the manual for some piece of equipment in your room once and you read the whole thing in less than an hour. When I came to visit you that afternoon, you recounted every detailed instruction on how to use it to me. Told me how to fix a dozen different problems that might arise with it.*

After that, you were obsessively curious about every piece of equipment in the lab. You wanted to know how the treadmill you always ran on worked. You wanted to know how the blood testing machines worked. You wanted to know how everything mechanical worked.

So I started swiping manuals for you. There was this filing cabinet in one of the offices where NovaTor kept them all. So every few days I'd sneak in and take one or two for you. You'd devour them instantly and impatiently wait for me to bring others.

The first time you remember meeting me was when I stole from Eden, but the first time I ever stole something was for you.

My eyes swept the page two or three times. I searched inside of myself, looking for that girl who liked to read boring instruction manuals. But if there was any tiny trace of her in there, I couldn't find her.

West was playing a game of tactics with me. He knew how desperately I wanted to remember my past, to understand who I was and why I had become the thing I was today. He was going to try and make me change my mind about choosing Avian by telling me all the stories of the two of us as children.

It wasn't going to work.

But I couldn't blame West for trying.

The next morning I found another note slipped under my door.

I fell asleep in your room once. I think we were probably about seven. I don't know if Dad or Grandpa forgot about me or what, but they left me there. The only time it ever happened.

But next thing I knew, you were sitting bolt upright in bed, screaming and crying that the walls were crushing in on you. I was pretty freaked out. Your emotional blockers were turned up full blast then and that was the most emotion I'd ever seen come from you. I mean, you were actually crying. The only time I've ever seen you cry.

When you saw I was still in the room, you hugged me and held on so tight I was covered in bruises the next day.

When Dad found me in the morning, he tried to take me back to our living quarters but you flipped out. You wouldn't let me leave.

I crumpled both of the notes and hid them in the back of my pants drawer. Bracing my hands on the dresser, I let my head hang in between my arms, my hair cascading around my face.

Like West had described in that nightmare from so long ago, it felt like the walls of this hospital were crushing in on me. West was a ghost that was present at all times. One that threatened to drown me and choke me from the inside out.

32

"Eve?"

My head jerked up to see Avian standing in the doorway, concern radiating off of him.

"Are you okay?" he asked.

"Yeah," I lied.

FIVE

"We're sweeping block eight today," Avian said. He stood at the front of the room next to Elijah. Avian drew a circle around the block on the map that hung on the wall before us. He capped the pen and turned back toward the crew.

"Tuck and the BRC cleared the bodies from there five days ago," Elijah spoke up. "Dr. Sun said that should be long enough for any communicable diseases from the bodies to die out. Still, it is recommended you wear a mask and throw in an antibody fogger before entering any buildings."

Bill started passing out small cans. Royce had developed them, with the help of Dr. Beeson's team. They could kill out any remaining organisms and keep us from contracting any diseases from the rotting Bane bodies.

Avian and Elijah's teams were doing a combined scout today.

"Let's move out," Avian said.

Avian insisted I work with the rehoming crew that day. I was going to go insane and he knew it. So for today, I would do something productive, even if the extra help wasn't needed. Regardless of how it made my chest constrict and the thought of living here forever.

We all filed out into the hall and toward the south entrance. We were nearly out the doors when West stepped into the lobby, dressed for duty.

So far I'd managed to avoid him in the twenty-four hours since his last note.

Avian fixed West with a grim expression and I couldn't seem to look at West.

"West has asked to join the rehoming crew," Elijah said in his rough voice. "Dr. Stone cleared him yesterday."

That was all the explanation Elijah gave. Because what else could he say?

I picked up my pace and moved to the front of our crew. I fell in next to Bill.

"Looks like this is about to turn into an awkward day," he said.

"Yeah."

I didn't look back as we headed for block eight. I had work to do and work was what I was good at.

Block eight was a solid looking row of apartments and two abandoned restaurants. They were older, but they seemed structurally sound. Window flower boxes hung from each unit, dried and scraggly looking plants lying dead in them.

"I want three soldiers to each unit," Elijah said loud enough the crowd would hear him. "Avian and I will take the commercial buildings."

I practically glued myself to Bill's side and pulled Nick into our circle. West met my eyes and shook his head. He turned to Graye and joined him and Raj.

Something heated under my skin and I swear, I could feel the tickle of a blackout in the back of my head.

"Let's go," Bill said, grabbing the collar of my jacket and dragging me toward the building. Balling my fists just once more, I turned and followed him and Nick toward a unit on the upper floor.

"You got this one?" Bill asked Nick.

He held up one of the cans and shook it violently to activate it. "On the count of three." Bill nodded, placing his hand on the door knob. "Three…" Nick counted. I held my shotgun ready, even though I knew there wouldn't be any Bane inside. Instinct dies hard. "Two… One…"

Bill pushed the door open a foot and Nick depressed the button on the top of the can and threw it inside. Bill yanked the door closed again.

Once the button was pushed on the antibody can you had exactly four seconds before it started fogging. Get locked in a room with one and you're dead.

We had to wait sixty seconds before we could enter the building. Nick watched the time tick away on his watch.

"How's Avian handling everything?" Bill asked quietly. Nick glanced up at us, but as usual for him, he remained silent.

"It's harder this time," I said, looking over the railing to the units below. "Avian got pretty pissed off when West got a little too close the other night. Royce was pretty angry too."

"That boy's going to have to learn to follow common sense someday," Bill said, shaking his head.

I didn't have a response. This entire situation was hard and I was quickly losing my cool when it came to West and his recovery. But I had in fact had feelings for West. Those weren't completely gone. I couldn't just hate West because I had decided I wanted to be with someone else.

These human emotions were too damn complicated.

"Time," Nick said as his watch beeped.

I pushed the door open and swept the space with my shotgun. It was perfectly empty though.

The building wasn't large. We entered a living area with simple furniture and carpeted floors. Just to the left was a small kitchen with molding food on the counter and an even smaller dining area with a table and four chairs.

"Looks pretty safe," Nick said as he walked around the space, testing his weight on the floor. Bill checked the kitchen.

I nodded, heading back for the doors that led off from the living room.

The door creaked when I pushed it open. I found a large bed, the sheets and blankets in a twisted mess in the middle of it. There was a dresser too large for the space. Sitting on it were three picture frames.

In one there was a picture with a smiling couple. She wore a flowing wedding dress, her hair in an elegant knot. He wore a handsome grey suit. They were looking at each other, their faces radiating love.

In another picture there was a little girl, probably younger than Brady. She had curly blond hair and wore a bright pink shirt. In the last picture there was a baby. The baby was young enough it was hard to tell if it was a boy or girl, but the pink blanket it lay on gave it away.

Swallowing hard, I checked the bedroom and bathroom attached to it. Everything looked safe.

There was one more door to check.

I pushed it open and stopped in the doorway.

The walls were painted a pale pink. A tiny bed was pushed into one corner. A frilly white blanket was tangled at the foot of it. A huge stuffed rabbit was about to fall off the edge. And in the opposite corner there was a crib. Toys sat neatly in bins along the walls. Sunlight shone in through the windows.

The room looked as if it was just waiting for those two little girls to come home and play.

"Everything good back here?" Nick asked, startling me.

"Yeah," I said, my voice sounding rough. "Let's go."

The three of us stepped back outside. Many of the other soldiers were already done. They stood in front of the building, talking and laughing, looking normal. Bill and Nick went to join them.

Seeing that pink room had shaken me. I thought of those little girls and how they'd had their life stolen from them. I thought about my own childhood, the one that had been stolen from me.

A hard knot formed in my stomach. I ducked around the building to try and find some quiet. The side road was littered with garbage and debris. I stepped over a trash can. I didn't want to be in my head just then.

I turned a corner into the back alley when I bumped right into someone. My bones instantly hissed to life and my breath snagged in my chest. I reached out a hand to steady myself, and pressed it right into the surface of West's inhibitor.

A scream leapt from my throat as I pulled my hand back. My hand looked deformed, as if all the bones in it had broken and magnetized themselves to the inhibitor.

West swore under his breath and reached out to steady me. "Are you okay?" he asked at the same time I shook out of his grasp.

"Stay away from me," I hissed, cradling my hand to my chest. The discomfort was dulling, my pain blockers kicking in. I could feel my bones trying to right themselves.

"Yeah, that's what everyone seems to be telling me these days," West said, a hard edge to his voice.

I looked up at him. His expression was angry, frightening even, now that his face was covered in so many scars.

"Look, West," I said, dropping my hand to my side. "I don't want things to have to be like this between us. But you've got to start thinking things through. You're pretty much the one person here who can kill me now. You've got to be more careful."

West suddenly chuckled as his gaze rose to the hazy blue sky and he shook his head. "Just think how romantically tragic this all would have been if you'd picked me instead of him. In love and wanting to be together, but you couldn't even touch me."

"West, stop it," I said, my voice dropping low as I sensed where he was going to take this.

"But instead, you get your happy ending," he said, his voice growing cold. He took a step toward me. His head dropped and he looked up at me from beneath his thick, dark lashes. "And what do I get?" He stopped a mere foot from me. My blood hissed. I stood with my back to the wall. "I get screwed!" West pounded his fist into the wall just to the left of my head. His nose was only six inches from mine.

"I get *infected* and you go and pick *him*?" he bellowed, his eyes growing darker by the second.

"I made my decision before I knew who was infected," I spat back as best I could. It felt as if my throat were closing up. I was struggling to breathe.

"What am I supposed to do now, Eve?" he said, his voice not softening in the slightest. "I'm supposed to live the rest of my life looking like a monster and watch you and him live out a happily ever after?"

"Back…" I struggled. "Back off, West."

"I don't think so," he said with a laugh in his voice. And for the first time in my life, I was afraid of West. "Not until you tell me that you don't love me. That the past doesn't matter."

"West…" I said. There were thick black spots swimming in my vision.

"Get off of her!" Avian bellowed and I heard feet pounding the road.

The next second an arm wrapped around West's throat and the two of them were tumbling across the pavement.

I collapsed to the ground, coughing violently. Avian rolled on top of West, pinning him to the ground. His fist connected with West's jaw, West's head sharply snapping to the left.

"Don't come near her again!" Avian threatened, landing another blow as West swung back.

West took a swing at Avian, which he blocked with his forearm before landing another punch to West's face.

"You have no idea who she really is!" West yelled. "She was never supposed to pick you! It was always me and her. Always!"

"That's enough!" Elijah shouted as he sprang for the two. He shoved Avian off of West while West tried for another swing. Bill darted into the alley, pulling Avian away, holding his arms pinned behind his back.

"I mean it!" Avian screamed. "You touch her again and I will kill you!"

I couldn't move, sitting immobile and stunned on the ground as I watched the mess I'd caused explode out of control.

What had I done?

What kind of an unfixable disaster had I created?

"All three of you back to the hospital, right now!" Elijah commanded, his eye wild and angry. "I will not have my own crew fighting amongst themselves!"

Avian jerked in Bill's arms, trying to get back at West, who stared at him with death in his eyes.

"That's enough!" I yelled, my ability to breathe returning.

"Cool it," Bill said, jerking when Avian lurched for West.

"Back to the hospital," Elijah growled again.

When Avian relaxed, Bill released him. Avian didn't look away from West as he shrugged his shoulders, adjusting the rifle on his back. His jaw flexed along with his fists as he turned and walked down the alley.

West shoved Elijah off of him and walked away in the opposite direction.

"You three need to get your crap together," Elijah snapped at me. "Your little love tiff is going to get someone killed."

SIX

"Welcome back."

I blinked, clearing the black, shifting lines from my vision.

The room hadn't even come into focus before Dr. Beeson wrapped the blood pressure cuff around my arm. It ticked as it filled, squeezing my arm.

"How do you feel?" he asked.

My heart beat erratically. My breathing came in shallow gulps. There must have been something physical inside of me, rising up, attempting to choke me, trying to drown me from the inside out.

All the guilt, shock, shame, everything I'd felt earlier, came crushing in on me tenfold.

"I..." I stuttered, overcome at the rushing feeling going on within me.

"Take a deep breath," Dr. Beeson said, his brows furrowing together. He pressed the stethoscope to my chest and listened to my heart crash against my rib cage. "Try to relax."

I made a small O with my lips and focused on my breaths.

This was my fourth emotional adjustment. This one was supposed to take my emotional blockers down to less than fifty percent.

"You seem overwhelmed," Dr. Beeson said, concern obvious in his voice. He lowered the stethoscope. "Your heart is racing and your blood pressure is up. Perhaps this was too big of a jump."

"No," I said, shaking my head. "It's okay. I need this."

"Is there a specific reason why?" he asked.

I opened my eyes and pulled myself into a sitting position. It felt like all of my insides had swelled and everything was trying to push its way up my throat to suffocate me.

"I'm going to hurt West if he keeps relapsing like this and I stay so emotionally unsympathetic." My vision blurred as I fixed my eyes on the floor. "Things are getting bad. I need to figure out how to deal with all this."

"I don't know that it has anything to do with your emotional blockers," Dr. Beeson said, glancing up at me from my chart. "This would be emotionally trying on anyone."

"Still," I said, shaking my head. I pulled my knees up to my chest and wrapped my arms around them. It made me feel slightly better, like maybe I wouldn't crack open and fall to pieces right there on the table. "I know I should try and talk to him again, to explain why I didn't choose him, but I know I'll screw it up and make things worse. Besides, he'll forget it all again soon."

"If this adjustment seems like too much, I want you to tell me right away," Dr. Beeson said, ignoring my last comment. What was he supposed to do? Give me relationship advice? "We have to be careful with this. We don't want to fracture you mentally. We could cause some serious damage."

"Serious damage," I said, shaking my head, giving a humorless chuckle. "Only I could get seriously damaged from becoming like everyone else."

"But you're not like everyone else," Dr. Beeson said, his voice lowering. "You are unique, Eve. You are special."

I didn't have anything to say to that. Accepting who, or rather what, I was had become a daily battle.

Suddenly a smile cocked in the corner of his mouth. "I still can't believe how much you look like your mother."

"How well did you know her?" I asked, glad for the distraction.

Dr. Beeson sat back in his seat, crossing his arms over his chest. "I only ever actually met her once. I was still in graduate school and was given the opportunity to tour the NovaTor facility. We ended up talking afterward. We met for dinner and ended up visiting for probably three hours."

"What was she like?" I asked.

A sad look flashed across his face, knowing he had enjoyed an opportunity I had been robbed of.

"She was whip-smart," he said, threading his fingers together in his lap. "Her attention to detail was impeccable. Her dedication to the development of TorBane was astounding. She was convinced it would save the world. She made me believe it would."

I had to swallow hard at that. I wasn't sure how I felt about it. My mother had helped develop TorBane, the technology that would destroy the world in a matter of months once it was made available to the public. She had helped develop the technology that made me less than human.

"How long was that before I was born?" I asked.

Dr. Beeson paused for a moment before he responded, as if calculating the time.

"I would suspect she was pregnant with you at that time," he said quietly. "She had said something about how she and her boyfriend had recently broken up."

An ache in my chest swelled.

My father. Who was he? What did he look like? Was he still out there somewhere? Was there any chance he was alive?

The worst part was that I knew I would never find the answers to my question.

I would never even know his name.

"That's enough for today," Dr. Beeson said. He placed his hand on my back. "I'm sorry, I shouldn't have brought your mother up. Not when you're like this."

"It's okay," I whispered, even though I wasn't sure it was.

"I'll call Avian to take you home, away from the hospital," he said, reaching for his radio. "I think it would be wise for you to have a few days to take it easy and adjust. Honestly, it sounds like you both could use some time away."

"You'll keep an eye on West for me?" I asked. Just saying West's name brought up a hurricane inside of me. "He's not in a good place right now."

"Of course."

Avian was not happy when he picked me up from Dr. Beeson's office. The three of us had argued for twenty minutes. Avian was insisting I shouldn't have to deal with being overwhelmed. I insisted that I was going to do something stupid if I didn't continue with my adjustments.

They finally got tired of arguing with me. Avian drove us to the beach.

But while the night progressed, I knew that maybe I was wrong. As we ate, I could feel this sense of regret, dread, and guilt building up inside of me.

The weight of the world seemed to be settling on my shoulders. The wreck I'd caused pressed in on my throat. Avian's reaction earlier had been because of my indecision.

Why couldn't I handle this? Why couldn't I be a normal person? Why was I so weak?

Avian was quiet and watched me, never saying a word.

When we were done with our dinner, I exited the tent and walked toward the water.

I stood with my toes in the sand, the salty waves lapping at them. I watched as the early December clouds gathered, growing heavy and dark. Electricity fizzed through the air, giving a sense of urgency to the world around me. A storm was gathering.

The air, the energy around and in me, the sense of needing to do something more, reminded me of the night the Bane had burned our gardens in the mountains to ash.

Wrapping my arms around myself, I rubbed my hands over my skin. Winter was upon us, and while it didn't have the bite and chill, or snow of old Eden, it was getting cooler. I'd soon be grateful for the warmth of the hospital, even though it would mean that I would be trapped within its walls for the next few months.

And I'd never be able to escape West there.

With the cities endless concrete walls, limitless broken roads, too many abandoned cars; I felt like a trapped animal.

For a moment I considered heading north. Far, far north. I'd seen maps before, knew that if I could travel far enough I'd find trees and forests again. Nature felt like home, in a way it was where I was born.

Somehow I didn't think this concrete jungle would ever feel like home.

Maybe we'd survive, if Avian and I just took off. We could find somewhere remote enough to outlast the Bane. We could take supplies with us, hunt for food. Maybe I could be happy again, feel free.

Then maybe West could move on.

But that was insane. Winter was at our door, food would be scarce. Temperatures would make it difficult to survive.

And what about Gabriel? Royce? Victoria, and Brady, and Lin, and Tuck?

And West?

I couldn't leave.

Home was wherever the people I cared about were. Home wasn't a dot on the map.

The soft crunch of sand behind me let me know Avian had stepped out of the tent. I took a few quick, deep breaths in attempt to calm myself down. I was getting worked up, my emotions too close to the surface.

Avian stopped at my side, his hands stuffed into his pockets. He didn't say anything, just stared out over the dark waters with his ever serious eyes.

I was grateful for Avian's silence. From the way he stood, the way he angled himself towards me just slightly, the way he kept pressing his lips together, I knew he could tell this adjustment had been too much. But he also had the sense to know when I just needed him there, even if he didn't say anything.

"What's on the other side?" I asked quietly, squeezing myself tighter as the temperature dropped a few more degrees. "What's across the water?"

"A whole lot of ocean, for a long ways," he said as he watched the lightning that started out far from the coast. "You'll start to see the curve of the Earth before you get to land. There are some scattered islands, but they're small. Then eventually you'll run into the Asian continent, Australia if you veer south."

"Do you think the Bane have gotten as bad in those places as they are here?" I asked.

"It's hard to imagine they haven't," he answered, his voice heavy and sad. "TorBane took hold worldwide within a few weeks."

49

I nodded. The wind started to pick up, fanning my hair behind me, making my breath catch in my throat.

"Maybe there's a place out there," I said, my eyes glazing over. Everything went blurry as my focus turned internal. "A place where the infection didn't travel to. One of those islands in a warm place. There'd be trees and sand, animals for hunting. It'd be safe."

Avian's arms wrapped around me from behind, his warmth sending a wave of goosebumps flashing across my skin.

"There is," he said, his lips close to my ear as he rested his chin on my shoulder. "That place is in each of us. It's what's kept us all going the last six years."

Something stung at the back of my eyes and I hated my human side for being weak. I couldn't vocalize that for the last few weeks I had felt like that place was disappearing for me.

As soon as I thought it, I knew how terrible and selfish that was. We'd won here in New Eden. We'd defeated the Bane and we'd found safety. At least for now. I had no right to complain or to be unhappy. I was alive and so were the people I cared about.

A flash of light let us know that the storm was moving closer to land and the clap of thunder followed just one second later.

Avian took my hand in his and led me back to the tent.

SEVEN

I inhaled slowly, leveling my eyes along the sight. And exhaling, I squeezed the trigger.

The old cup lid I'd tacked up on the outside wall of the long forgotten about house exploded as I hit it dead center. I was having a good time with Avian's gift.

"Perfect," Avian said. I glanced over at him to find a wide smile on his face. He'd started smiling so much more since the Pulse went off. "Not that I'd expect anything less from you."

"Weapons and shooting are easy," I said as I refilled the magazine. "It's people that are difficult. This is just calculation and a good eye."

A can that lay discarded on the ground down the road jumped into the air as I hit it.

"I wonder if we could make an arrow with an explosive head," I said as I watched Avian take aim with his new bow. "An arrow alone might not be enough to take down a Bane, but you make it explosive, and if you can embed it in their chest or something, and you'd take them out for sure."

"Sounds like an afternoon of fun for Royce," Avian said as he released the arrow.

It would be. There might not be any Bane around at the moment, but that didn't keep Royce from making all kinds of new toys of mass destruction. As a former weapons specialist, he had the deranged creativity to create anything, if he could only get his hands on the resources.

"You hungry?" Avian asked, embedding yet another perfect shot. I still wasn't used to seeing him handle weapons, and even more so, use them so accurately. Avian was a better shot than I was with a bow.

"Ugh," I groaned. "I need to go hunting. I can't stand any more of this canned and last-forever food they have here."

Avian chuckled. "Yeah, I'll admit, I miss our gardens so much it hurts some days. What I wouldn't do for a few fresh tomatoes or a handful of strawberries."

"Don't remind me," I growled, placing my Desert Eagle in the holster at my hip. "That's cruel."

Shouldering his bow, Avian took my hand in his and we slowly made our way back to the beach.

The wind had finally died out after raging all night. The tent had flapped and whipped around, the stakes were yanked out of the ground. The only thing that kept it from blowing away was the weight of our bodies.

Neither of us had gotten much sleep that night. But at least we weren't caged up in the hospital.

By morning I was feeling better, or at least I didn't feel like I was getting overwhelmed by everything going on inside of me.

Avian set to building a fire to cook our meager meal and I stashed our weapons beneath our cots. It was an impressive hoard of firepower I'd been building. I had another stockpile in the closest house that looked out over the water. The Bane were gone, for now, but that didn't mean I let my guard down.

I stepped back outside and watched as Avian started cooking our meal.

"You were pretty aggressive with West yesterday," I said, not wanting to talk about the event, but knowing it had to be addressed.

Avian grunted, but didn't look up from the fire. His expression darkened.

"Want to tell me what that was about?" I asked. "I've never seen you like that."

He sighed, placing a pan over the fire and dumping some kind of substance into it. When he was finished he stayed where he was, kneeling on one knee.

"I keep losing people," he said, finally meeting my eye. "I lost all my commanding officers, my fellow soldiers. Then I had to shoot my own parents to save Sarah. Then Tye got infected. Given that one was my own fault."

I shook my head, about to argue that he couldn't have known Tye would get infected because of a request he made, but Avian plowed on. "And then Sarah dies of something I can't cure."

He ran a hand over his short hair, his mouth pulling downward in a frown. He shook his head and I noticed then that he was trembling just slightly. I crossed to kneel by him in the sand. I put a hand on either side of his face, drawing his eyes to mine.

"You're all I have left, Eve," he said, his voice husky and low. "I will do anything—anything—to keep something from happening to you. I'm tired of being the calm one who always fixes things. I'm not going to sit back and watch West hurt you."

"I know," I said quietly, searching his eyes. There was regret in them. I knew he wasn't proud of what he'd done. But there was also desperation. I felt it too.

I pressed my lips to his. All the hurt and pain and confusion slowly melted away as his hand came up to my hair, pulling me closer.

"Avian, Eve," a familiar voice called from up by the road. I turned to see Tuck walking up on the beach, an unfamiliar electric car parked on the road at the edge of the sand.

"What are you doing here?" I asked. No one other than Elijah and Gabriel had ever come to the tent.

"Royce sent me after you two," Tuck said. The alarm in his eyes outweighed the embarrassed flush in his cheeks at catching us together. "Some new people showed up today."

"How many?" Avian asked, his expression dark and serious again.

"Twenty," Tuck said. "They're well-armed and seem to know how to handle themselves."

"Twenty?" I said, not hiding my shock. "Where did they come from?"

"That's what's got Royce and Gabriel so worried," he said. "They won't say. But they arrived by Coast Guard ship early this morning, just north of here. They've been asking a lot of questions but not answering any."

"Okay," I said, turning back to Avian. He gave a little nod, his eyes carrying a sad look, like he knew how much I didn't want to go back into the city yet—that in reality—I wasn't quite ready. "We'll head out in just a minute."

Tuck nodded and jogged back toward the electric car.

"You ready to go back?" Avian asked, tucking a stray strand of hair behind my ear.

"Are you?" I asked and instantly the air grew heavy.

"I think it's best if I just avoid West for a while," he said. His gaze fell to the sand beneath us.

"Hey," I said, my brow furrowing. "What is it?"

"I trust you, okay? Don't get me wrong there. But just promise me that you'll always be honest with me."

I shook my head. "You know I will," I said, attempting to push back the black feelings trying to rise up in my blood. "What's this really about?"

He took a moment to respond and I could feel his turmoil. "I know that you have mixed emotions about West," Avian said. "You still have some kind of feelings about him and I wouldn't expect that to immediately go away. You two have some kind of history that I can never be a part of. I get that. Just…always be honest with me about it, okay?"

He pulled me into his chest and wrapped his arms around me. I laid my head on his chest, listening for the beat of his heart, the sound that was the anchor to my world.

"The honest truth is this," I said, looking up into his eyes. "I love you. You are who I want and need to be with. That's never going to change."

As we parked the motorcycle in the underground parking garage, Avian tucked a small handgun into his belt beneath his shirt. I checked my Desert Eagle, making sure I could pull it out quickly in case I needed it. I had no doubt a lot of members of New Eden would be packing with these newcomers.

The stairs echoed back our footsteps as we climbed the two sets of flights to the main level of the hospital. A gust of warm air caressed my face when we stepped out onto the main floor.

I bumped the door into Graye as we entered. There were no civilians in the lobby, which was odd considering this was the main hub of all operations of New Eden. Instead I found Elijah and the majority of his and Avian's crew, as well as all of Tuck's team guarding doors and stairways with loaded weapons.

In the middle of the room stood twenty people I didn't know, their pale faces and bodies hardened by the world we lived in. They held their own weapons.

"What's going on?" I whispered to Graye.

"They're refusing to tell Gabriel or Royce much of anything. They want to talk with Royce privately but Elijah isn't having it, not without Avian here. He wants someone here in charge of security detail."

"And you and Bill are useless?" I asked in an annoyed voice.

Graye shrugged, shaking his head in exasperation.

"Finally," Royce suddenly said, spotting Avian and me. "Elijah, happy now?"

Elijah nodded his scarred head.

"You two, come with us," Royce said, pointing at two people in the front of this new group with the tip of his AK-47. "Avian, Eve, care to join us?"

I nodded, as did Avian. Royce, Gabriel, the two newcomers, Avian, and I all wedged ourselves into the elevator.

"Anyone makes a wrong move, don't hesitate to shoot," Royce said as the silver doors slid closed.

"This is how you treat your guests?" the woman asked, her voice hard and mocking.

"Forgive us if our manners are a little rusty," Royce barked. "But when you come into our city armed like this with no answers, we don't serve up the welcome cookies and milk."

The elevator dinged and we walked down the hall toward the conference room. I felt uneasy that we were only one floor below the blue level, where the most valuable devices and people in the world resided.

As soon as everyone was in the room, I positioned myself in front of the door and Avian stood in front of the window.

"We could start with some names," Royce said, bracing his hands on the table, staring them down with his steely eyes.

"Margaret," the woman said, leaning forward as if to prove Royce didn't intimidate her.

"Alistar," the man beside her said.

"Good," Royce said with a cocky smile. "That's better. Because when you walk into our town, you answer our questions. You heard our radio message."

"Yes," Margaret replied, folding her hands over one another on the table. "Your message did promise food, shelter, a home."

"Somehow I don't get the feeling that's what you're really looking for here," Royce growled. "You don't go begging for a bed armed like this."

"We've never heard of another group surviving in such large numbers," Gabriel butted in. I sensed his attempt to smooth things over. Gabriel was always the peacekeeper but knew when to not let things get out of hand. "We're just surprised at your numbers."

"Where are you from?" Royce asked. I could tell this wasn't the first time he'd asked these two this question.

"Where are any of us from?" Margaret said back. "Like you, we're from everywhere. Just trying to survive in an impossible world."

"That isn't an answer," Royce said, leaning forward again, his voice icy.

This game was tiring me very quickly and I was having a very bad week. The distrust and anger inside of me quickly flooded my veins.

I crossed the room and nestled the barrel of my rifle between her ribs. "Where are you from?" I said.

She jumped, much to my satisfaction, and her face blanched all the more white.

Good. She was still capable of feeling fear.

"North," she said, her voice a little too loud. "We've been in the forests up north. We've been hiding there for the past year."

"The Redwoods?" Avian asked, studying them.

Margaret nodded.

"We heard the message," Margaret said, now fixing me with hard eyes. I stepped back to the door now that she was talking. "We were curious to talk to other survivors, so we came. We weren't exactly expecting to be held hostage."

"One can never be too careful these days," Royce said, standing straight again. He was still tense, but I felt him backing down now that they had answered some of his questions.

"We're not looking to join you permanently," Alistar said, looking around at each of us. "We just wanted to talk, share information. We thought it could be valuable."

Royce glanced over at Gabriel who shrugged and shook his head as if to say it was Royce's call.

"Everyone will be heading to bed right now," Royce said. I glanced out the window that overlooked the buildings around us. The sun had dipped below the skyline and darkness was settling. "We'll talk in the morning. Avian, Gabriel, will you take their group to the fourth floor?"

They both nodded and directed Margaret and Alistar back toward the elevator.

I almost smiled when Royce said the fourth floor. It was the former mental unit. Very secure. Easy to lock down.

Royce didn't trust these people any more than I did.

When they were out in the hall, Royce shut the door and turned to me.

"I'm shutting down all the elevators when they're settled," he said, meeting my eyes and crossing his arms over his chest. "I want you guarding the blue floor. All the scientists will be sleeping on that floor tonight. We're not saying anything about the Pulse, the Extractor, you, or West until we know more about these people. Got it?"

"Yes, sir," I said with a nod.

"Don't shoot me, Eve," he said as I turned to leave. "But I think it's best if West stays up there tonight as well. It's a little obvious just looking at him that he's had some major work."

I gave him a hard stare for a long moment. But in the end logic won out, and I couldn't argue with him.

"Make sure Avian knows where I am tonight," I said as I walked toward the stairs.

"Yes ma'am."

The scientists didn't even begin to argue when I told them we were all in lockdown for the night. Half of them slept up on the blue floor more than they slept in their own rooms anyway. Many of them had become anti-social after all the years they had spent holed up on the blue floor working on the Pulse. A lot of them didn't know how to mingle with the general population any more.

Thankfully I could always count on Dr. Beeson to feel guilty about what he'd helped do to me, and he kept West occupied while I stood guard at the door to the stairs that led access to the rest of the hospital.

The floor grew quiet as everyone settled down for the night. The lights along the floor, running through the walls, glowed brilliant as ever. I positioned myself with an assault rifle in front of the door to the staircase.

There was something about what Margaret and Alistar had said that didn't sit right with me. They were from north of us. But not far enough north that they wouldn't see the sun on a nearly daily basis. They, as well as the rest of their group, had been white and pasty-faced. I looked down at my own arms. Even though I'd been inside quite a bit the last two months, my skin was still well tanned from the sun.

I wondered how big their lies really were.

EIGHT

"Any idea what's going on down there?"

I turned to find West behind me, hands stuffed into his pockets. My eyes immediately fell to the blue glow coming through his shirt.

"No," I responded and turned back to the door leading to the stairwell.

The sun had risen. It was now eight o'clock and the blue floor had yet to receive an update.

"Royce must really not trust them if he's hiding all of us up here," West said. I heard him sit on the floor against the wall.

"There's something not right about them," I said. I blinked hard.

I wasn't tired. I was used to staying up at nights and keep guard. This was second nature to me. This was what I was good at.

But my eyes were burning from staring at that stupid door all night.

"You look like crap," he said.

"I could say the same thing," I snapped. "But that would be mean."

"Cold, Eve," he said. "Not that I don't somewhat deserve it."

"Somewhat?"

"I'm not going to make this easy for you," he said in a low voice.

I could tell he wanted me to look back at him, but I wasn't going to give him the satisfaction. He needed to face reality.

I was trying with West. I really was.

"Lock down is over." Dr. Beeson was in the hall, a radio in his hand. "They're calling everyone down for a meeting in the auditorium."

I didn't like it, it felt dangerous to gather us all into one room, but I didn't exactly have the power to override Royce.

Everyone from the blue floor made their way down the stairway and we all exited onto the second floor.

I'd only ever been in the auditorium once before. It was a massive room that dropped down at an angle toward a stage. Rows upon rows of seats rose up from the elevated stage. The room would easily seat five hundred people.

As soon as I entered the room, Avian and Elijah signaled to me from just to the side of the stage.

"What's going on?" I whispered as I joined them. I was on instant alert when I realized they were keeping to the shadows, out of view of the masses.

"We still didn't get any answers this morning," Avian said, his eyes scanning those who filtered into the room. "They mostly just asked a lot of questions. We told them

63

about the Pulse since they basically already knew about it being as they walked into a cleared city. No one is too worried about them stealing it. It doesn't exactly fit into your back pocket."

"They're saying they'd like to stay a while, talk some more, tell us what it's like up north," Elijah said. He held a rifle tight in his hands. "They're asking that we let them stay for a week."

"I don't like it," I whispered, shaking my head. My eyes fell on Margaret, who sat in the front row. She had the tips of her fingers pressed together, her gaze fixed on the empty stage.

"Neither does Royce," Elijah said. "That's why he's having security detail quietly follow them at all times. They know we're going to be watching them. But not how closely."

"Why doesn't Royce just ask them to leave?" I asked. By this point it looked like most everyone had entered the room.

"Because none of us want a war to start," Avian said.

Royce and Gabriel stepped onto the stage.

"Take the right exit," Elijah said, pointing back toward the door I'd entered through. "Keep a low profile."

I nodded and quietly slipped back up the stairs to the door. I kept my rifle hanging at my left side so that it was out of sight, but was ready to use it at one wrong move.

"Thank you all for coming," Royce said as he turned his eyes out on those before him. "I am sure you are all wondering what the dramatics have been about the last twenty-four hours."

The members of New Eden looked frightened, glancing around at those they did not recognize. Brady hung tight around Victoria's neck, Wix with his arms around her. Lin sat next to a few other women, each eying the strangers.

"We've been honored with a surprise visit from our friends to the north," Royce said. Even from a distance, I could see how he clenched his teeth. "They heard our radio broadcast and came to learn more about our way of life. They will be staying on the fourth floor for the next seven days." There was an underlying tone that said they would not be welcome after seven days.

"You are welcome to talk to them if you like, but I won't feel bad if you don't feel compelled to get to know these people who will be leaving our presence in a week. But I wanted to let you all know what was going on," Royce said.

"Please let your friends and neighbors know," Gabriel said, stepping forward. "Not everyone is in attendance today, so we don't want anyone feeling alarmed when they see strangers in our city."

"Back to life, people," Royce said with a wave of his arms, dismissing everyone.

Most everyone looked at least slightly wary and confused but they all filed back out of the auditorium. Royce and Gabriel stayed behind with Margaret and Alistar, but Elijah once again signaled to Avian and me.

We all quickly made our way to room 112, center of security.

Bill, Graye, and the other dozen soldiers on security detail were already gathered. I did however notice West was not joining us. Elijah must have finally realized having him mix with the crew was a bad idea for now.

"Royce wants us to tail these people for the next week. That means twenty-four-seven. Raj and Nick, you'll be on night watch," Elijah said, pointing to the two of them. "I want a guard in the staircase, and another at the elevator. They'll know there's someone at the elevator, but we're not telling them about the staircase. Royce wants to test them and see if they're going to sneak out at night and go snooping around.

"The rest of you will each be assigned a floor. Bill, Graye, and Banner, you three will cover the grounds around the hospital. Anyone leaves, you tail them. Call for back up if they spread more than the three of you can keep an eye on."

"Dr. Beeson will be bringing hand-held radios any moment for each of you. You're to check in on an hourly basis. They will report directly back to myself and Royce. I don't have to say that if you see something suspicious, you report it immediately."

"I really don't like this," I said once again under my breath.

"Yeah," Avian said back. "I think everyone has a bad feeling about this."

I was torn between duty and curiosity.

Avian and I were in charge of watching the first floor, from the time we woke, until the time the newcomers were herded back to the fourth floor at night.

My assignment was to watch. To make sure nothing happened, that no one got out of line.

But I wanted to know what was going on.

Margaret and Royce spent most of their time on the sixth floor, in his office. Elijah stood constant guard alone just outside Royce's door.

I wanted to know what they were talking about. I wanted to make sure Royce didn't spill our secrets, even though I trusted him not to. I wanted to hear what was happening to the world outside of New Eden.

But I wouldn't abandon my duties.

I finally had a job.

I hung back in the lobby, watching. We'd moved the elementary and other school classes to the empty third floor. While Lin and the other teachers conducted class an armed guard stood watch over them. The dozen people who were employed in the operation of New Eden worked as usual in the lobby, but these outsiders slowly wandered, watching, asking questions.

I was proud of those around me. They were careful. They watched what they said.

But I had a bad feeling that eventually someone was going to slip up.

I looked up when West stepped into the lobby. West met my gaze for a moment when he spotted me. He shook his head nearly imperceptibly before his attention turned to the outsider who approached him.

I watched very carefully as West talked.

I'd had trust issues with West ever since the day I caught him stealing food from Eden. But back then those trust issues had only been important between the two of us.

Could I still trust him to keep our people and our secrets safe?

By the fifth day, I was so agitated I could hardly stand it. I felt cooped up and blind. I felt in the dark and out of the loop.

"You okay?" Avian asked as we switched places. We took shifts, either at the front of the hospital, with the lobby and restrooms, or the back, with the kitchens and medical wing.

"I just want them to leave," I said, my eyes sweeping the hallway.

"Two more days," he said quietly. He placed his hand on the back of my head and pressed a kiss to my brow.

"I can't stand this," I said, shaking my head. "I need out. I need trees and mountains. I need—"

"Hey," Avian cut me off, pulling me into his arms. "It's okay."

"No," I said. It felt like something wild and dangerous was in my throat, quickly rising up, choking me. "It's not. I need out. I can't breathe."

"Whoa," Avian said, stepping back just a bit so he could look down into my face. "Eve, if you need a break, I'm sure we could tell Elijah. He'll find someone to fill in."

"I don't need a break," I said, my voice sounding disgusted. I instantly felt ashamed at myself. "Forget what I said. I'm…fine."

"Eve, you're obviously *not* fine," he said, concern flooding his face. "You've been on the verge of a lash-out for the last week. It's understandable that moving into the city and having all these adjustments would be hard on you."

I shook my head, the back of my eyes stinging. My line of sight rose to the ceiling and I couldn't look back at Avian because I felt so disgusted with myself. "I am not that weak. I am not that human."

"Eve," Avian said, his voice hard and stern. It took me off guard enough to meet his eyes again. "You *are* human. And it is *okay*."

"I'm going to talk to Dr. Beeson," I said, taking a step away from him, my eyes falling to the floor this time. "This last adjustment was too much. You two were right. I can't handle any more of these."

Avian stopped short. Everything in his posture and stance said that he didn't know what to say.

Gathering myself, I turned and headed back toward the kitchen.

An hour after the outsiders went to bed, I lied down, staring up at the dark ceiling. I was working very hard to not think or feel anything.

My door opened but I didn't bother turning to see who it was. A warm body slipped into the bed next to me, strong arms circling my waist. I numbly turned on my side and rested my head on Avian's chest.

"I understand how hard you are trying to be empathetic with West," he said in a low voice. "And how you're trying your best to be like the rest of us. I know you're trying to understand the crazy emotions we all have to deal with."

He pressed his lips into my hair, gathering me tighter against his body. He took several deep breaths and I realized the way I had been behaving the last week had not been hard on me alone.

"But you seem to think that you need to rediscover who you are now that you know the truth about your origins."

He pulled away from me slightly so he could meet my eyes. His own burned with intensity. "Eve, there is nothing wrong with who you are. With the way you are. You are you, Eve, and not anyone else. You're tough and you're stubborn, and you don't always understand emotions and what you or everyone else is feeling, but that is part of who you are.

"I fell in love with a girl who was okay with not fully understanding her past. I fell in love with a girl who stood on her own and owned her present and future. *That* is who you are, Eve. You don't need to be anyone else, for anyone else."

For the second time in my life, I felt a bead of moisture rolling down my cheek.

Not because Avian had made me sad or hurt my feelings.

But because I had never had that much acceptance of myself. I had never thought someone could fully love me the way I was—twisted, manipulated, and engineered.

He was right. I didn't need to rediscover who I was. I didn't need to change into someone different. That was betraying myself. That was the worst kind of self-loathing I could imagine.

I pressed my forehead to Avian's and breathed for a moment, emotions swelling in my chest. This time, I didn't mind them.

"I am not me without you," I said. "Thank you for always standing by my side."

Avian brushed his lips against mine. His hand pressed into the back of my neck, his fingers tangling in my hair.

It took a man capable of an immeasurable amount of understanding to strip away the insecurities I'd felt after learning what I was. It took a man capable of loving me until the end of the world to make me accept myself.

And I would move heaven and hell to keep him.

Always.

I breathed a little easier the next morning. I just had to survive today and tomorrow and then these outsiders would leave.

And then Dr. Beeson would have time to fix me. To make me me again. And maybe I wouldn't have a nuclear meltdown.

Avian and I switched places, he headed for the lobby, and I started for the kitchen.

I was about to walk into the dining area when I heard two voices followed by a laugh, and froze. I ducked just outside of the doorway and listened.

"Come on," a female voice said. "You did not get scars like that falling out of a truck."

Even though she was asking about a heavy subject, her voice was light, like she was amused at the conversation.

It could only be Elijah or West who would answer, and I knew exactly where Elijah was and that wasn't down here in the dining area.

"Are you calling me a liar?" West responded.

"Yeah," the girl said with a laugh. "I guess I am."

"Maybe I'm Frankenstein's monster," he said. I could almost see the way he would raise his eyebrow at her.

"You're pretty scary looking," she said. "But not quite that scary."

"I am a monster," he said, his tone growing more serious. "Just not that kind."

Hot urgency burned through my veins. I wasn't going to sit and listen to this anymore. I stormed into the dining area and over to their table. I barely glanced at the girl he sat with. I grabbed West by the front of his thick shirt and hauled him out into the hall and into a closet.

"You need to be more careful," I said between clenched teeth. "You're going to expose us all."

"Get off me, Eve," he said, his voice escalating as he tried to shove me. I didn't budge.

I had him pinned against the shelves, my forearm across his shoulders.

"Royce doesn't want them knowing about the Extractor," I said, my eyes burning into his. "And you're about to blow that."

"It's a little difficult keeping that secret, walking around looking like this," he said. "And hiding this." He ripped his button up shirt open, exposing his inhibitor through the thin white shirt he wore underneath.

"Stay away from them if you have to," I said, backing off because my bones were starting to splinter being so close to West.

"No," he said indignantly. "I am not going to lock myself up in some room because you can't stand the sight of me actually talking to another woman."

"Oh my gosh," I said, not able to help rolling my eyes. "We so need to get over this. This is a lot bigger than our little love triangle past."

West shook his head and stormed out of the closet.

I stood in the dark for a moment, trying to pull in the wild pieces that seemed to be breaking off of me.

Avian was right. I was on the verge of a break down, and I was going to hurt someone.

And I knew who that someone would be.

The second these people left, I'd have Dr. Beeson fix me.

Because I didn't know how to function as a human. I was part Bane, and I was finally ready to accept that.

NINE

"All units to the auditorium."

The radio crackled to life, static for just a moment, followed by a harsh, demanding voice. Royce.

I shot out of bed, adrenaline flooding my system. For a moment I was back in my tent, ready to track a Bane down through the woods, shotgun in hand.

"What'd that just say?" Avian asked groggily in the dark.

"All units to the auditorium," I repeated, my pants already pulled on and tying the laces on my boots. "It was Royce."

I was impatient, waiting for Avian's sleepy self to get ready to move. We both jogged down the hall toward the auditorium, each of us with a rifle in one hand, a handgun in another pocket. Avian's necklace bounced softly on my chest as we ran.

We stepped into the dimly lit space and found what looked to be every one of the outsiders gathered on the stage. Raj, Nick, Elijah, and Royce all surrounded them, guns pointed in their directions.

Half a dozen other soldiers burst into the auditorium the same time Avian and I did, and we joined those on the stage.

"What's going on?" I asked at the same time as Bill.

"This one was trying to sneak out through the stairway," Raj said in his heavy accent, pointing to one of the outsiders. "He was trying to get to the roof with that." He pointed to a small black box that sat in the middle of the stage. It was maybe six inches by six inches.

"What is it?" I asked.

"They're not saying," Royce said, his jaw so tight I thought his teeth might crack. His eyes blazed and every muscle in his body was flexed. He looked ready to kill someone.

Dr. Beeson suddenly appeared in the doorway and jogged down the stairs.

"Is this it?" he asked, pointing to the box when he reached the stage.

"That's what he was trying to get to the roof," Raj said with a nod.

Dr. Beeson crossed to the box, and carefully picked it up. He lifted a lid and his face was illuminated with a flashing green light.

"Bomb?" Graye asked, automatically taking a step back.

Dr. Beeson's face paled, but he shook his head. He tipped the box and something small slipped out into his hand.

It was a two inch, silver cylinder. A green light flashed at the top of it every two seconds.

"If I'm not mistaken," Dr. Beeson said with a shaking voice. "It's a beacon."

"A beacon?" Avian said. "What kind of beacon?"

"You built a beacon to call out the Bane?" Royce bellowed. Something hot and wild flashed across his eyes. He slammed the butt of his gun to the back of Alistar's head. He collapsed in a limp heap.

Instantly, everyone was drawing weapons and two handguns and a crossbow were pointed in my own direction.

"You better start talking," Elijah said through clenched teeth. "Or this is going to turn into a blood bath."

"Alright," Margaret said, closing her eyes for a moment and taking a deep breath. "You have your devices and we have ours. Together we could clear the entire west coast."

"And you were what? Just going to set off your beacon and hope we'd power up the Pulse for you to wipe out the Bane that would come flooding into the city?" Royce growled.

"You have a device that could save the rest of humanity and you aren't using it," she said, turning cold, hard eyes on him.

"We don't even know that it will work again," he growled. "It requires an astronomical amount of power that has to be built up over days. If you'd set that thing off tonight, you would have killed us all."

"Surely you have it ready should the need for it arise," she said, her voice disbelieving.

"It isn't something easily turned on and off on a whim," Dr. Beeson said.

"Are you really so comfortable here in your little city that you think it safe to let your defenses down?" Margaret scoffed.

"You'll leave as soon as it is light outside," Royce growled.

"We are not done discussing this matter," Margaret answered.

"Trust me, we are."

"And how are you certain that this is the only beacon we brought with us?" she asked. "How do you know we didn't plant another before you found us?"

Royce crossed through the group and roughly grabbed Margaret's arm. "You're coming with me. The rest of you, keep them here."

I met the eyes of the girl whom West had been talking with.

My stomach disappeared when a slow smile curled on her lips.

We stood like that, for two hours. Guns and crossbows and even bows and arrows pointed at each other.

No one dared utter a word, for fear of setting everyone off.

Finally, a voice crackled over the radio.

"All newcomers are to be taken out the south entrance of the hospital." Royce. He said no more.

"I want you to move out, single file," Elijah said in his rough voice. "Out that door, down the hall, and through the south doors. Nick, take the lead."

My entire body tensed when all the outsiders looked at us for a long moment. There was indecision in their eyes, like they weren't sure if they should do as they were told, or stay and fight.

I didn't relax though when they started following in a careful line behind Nick out the door. I glanced over at Avian once before I followed along the line. He just nodded.

One by one, we walked down the hall, descended the stairs, and out the front doors.

We stopped outside the hospital, and waited for orders.

Margaret's form appeared in the door. Followed by Royce.

He had a gun pressed square to the back of her head.

"What's going on?" an outsider yelled. Half of them stepped forward.

I pressed the barrel of my shotgun to a man's chest and shook my head. "I suggest you don't move."

"The lot of you will leave this city immediately!" Royce shouted so all would hear him. "You will head out now or I will shoot her right here."

A shot rang out. Royce darted to the left, rolling on the ground as Margaret dashed forward.

I turned, my barrel scanning the crowd around me.

Margaret and a few of her men had turned down the road and were sprinting west.

I took off after them, my shotgun leveled.

There was a decision to make in that moment. Did I shoot them dead and become a murderer but keep them from possibly murdering us? Or did I show mercy and risk them flooding our city with Bane?

They cut around a corner, killing the choice.

"Eve!" I heard Avian shout from behind me.

I turned just briefly enough to see him knock a man unconscious with the butt of his shotgun and take off after me.

"I got this!" I bellowed, kicking up my speed.

I turned the corner and faltered for just a moment. Margaret was in sight. But her men were gone.

Something embedded itself into my side and every muscle in my body locked up. Air froze in my lungs, and black lines flickered across my vision. I hit the ground like a freshly cut tree. Across the street and just around the corner, I could see Avian, his fist connecting with another man's jaw.

I rolled as I hit the ground, my vision turning up to the cloudy sky. A man's face entered my field of vision. He had something in his hands and everything in me wanted to fight back as he covered my head with it.

But then everything shut down.

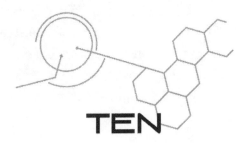

TEN

The ground was moving and it made my stomach sick.

A quick tug upward, and then a stomach dropping downward motion. Repeat.

Over and over I bobbed.

I was on water.

My eyes felt like sandpaper as I tried to pull them open. Everything was black and blur. And I couldn't find my body. I was aware that it was still there, but it may as well have been dead. Nothing could move.

I could however hear feet shuffling. They sounded like they were behind a door maybe. Muffled.

Air couldn't move past my dead lips, couldn't cry out for answers. Or help.

Suddenly, there were voices.

"You really think this doctor of yours can fix me?"

Something inside of me died when I recognized that voice.

West.

"He was the best heart surgeon there was on the West Coast before the Evolution."

And instantly I was full of fire and wrath.

That was the girl he'd been talking to in the dining area.

"I just hope this wasn't a mistake," he said, his voice growing quieter. "Cause I'm a dead man if he can't take that scrap out."

The pieces of the puzzle started sliding into place with only a few words.

I calculated in my head the amount of time West had. I got the sense we'd left New Eden and were headed back to wherever these people were from. I couldn't gauge how long we'd been traveling. But it had been just over a week from the time West came out of Extraction to the time before I got knocked out.

West only had about five days. Seven if he was really lucky.

He really was a dead man if this supposed doctor couldn't fix him.

Had my harshness toward him really driven him to do this? To betray his family and look for an elusive fix?

But I also had to consider why I was here, drugged and bound. I couldn't imagine anyone else would have given away my secret. Had West traded it for the surgery? Had they tricked it out of him? Had he let it slip?

"Don't look so down," the female voice said. "You made the right choice."

"I know I needed away from her," West's voice grew quieter. "But I just feel weird about leaving everyone. About leaving her. I searched for her for five years, and now I'm just walking away."

"You made the right choice," she said again, her words starting to slur in my ears.

Shadows started climbing in my brain, heavy and thick. I tried to keep them out, to find a door to close to them. But they were fog and mist and they crept in through all the cracks in my head.

***

There was light dancing behind my eyelids. It was dull and gray. But it was light.

"A little too effective," a voice said. "Wouldn't you say?"

"Yes ma'am," another responded, shame and fear in it.

"See if you can rouse her." The voice was female.

Something hard and cold whipped my head sharply to the left. But the rest of my body held firmly in place.

My eyes flashed open.

The outsiders were gathered around me, Margaret at the forefront of them all. Alistar stood at her side and another man with a gun stood just to the side of me. It was him that had just woken me with the butt end of his rifle.

I was bound to what looked like a moving-dolly with heavy chains. I tried jerking my arms, but didn't move an inch. I wasn't going anywhere.

We were all on a boat. A very large boat. We were bobbing just twenty yards from the shore.

And sitting right on that shore was a massive, towering city.

"This doesn't exactly look like the Redwoods," I growled as my eyes met Margaret's.

"We lied," she said, that grin creeping across her face. "Welcome to Seattle."

"What about New Eden?" I asked, red hot coals building in me.

"Fine, for the most part," she said, her expression going dark. "Once we realized what a valuable asset you were, we decided to take what we could and cut our losses. We don't have the Pulse, but I'm sure you'll provide some very interesting, very valuable information."

"I don't know anything about how to build the Pulse," I said through gritted teeth. "And I'm not telling you anything."

"That's not exactly what we're after," she said with that wicked grin of hers. "And talking wasn't the method I had in mind to obtain it."

"Where's West?" I demanded, again trying to jerk out of my bonds.

"He and some of the others headed for shore just before dawn on the speed boat," she answered. "He's safe."

"What did you promise him?"

"We'll honor our promise," she said, lifting her chin just a bit, as if I had insulted her integrity. "He provided valuable information, even if he didn't realize he was giving it and what we intended to do with it."

"You tricked it out of him," I said, hatred spewing from my every word.

The grin spread on her face and there was a manic look in her eyes. "The poor boy was so starved for some female attention. Tara was so attentive and such a good listener.

She was so willing to hear all about the emotionally broken girl who picked another man over him."

"He doesn't know you've taken me, does he?" I said, my voice growing quieter.

"We thought it best with his…condition, if he remained cooperative and calm. You wouldn't want him making any rash decisions, would you? We just might not be able to help him if he becomes unpleasant. And you might not have picked him, but I am sure you still don't want him Evolving."

I knew then that I would have no choice but to cooperate with this witch.

She saw it in my face and I wanted to kill her when that smile of hers reached her eyes.

"Now then," she said turning to look at the shore. "We need your help I'm afraid. This big ship didn't move as fast as we would have liked it to. We sent ahead some of our crew on the speed boat, including your West. They should have gotten to safety before the Bane woke. But it's starting to get light, and they're waiting for us."

She pointed to the shore and I finally noticed the small details I had missed before.

Bane.

At least a dozen of them standing along the shore, watching us with empty eyes.

"From what your friend told Tara, you have the ability to control them," she looked back at me with curiosity. "We need you to keep them off us so we can get home."

I chuckled and shook my head. "I think you're overestimating my abilities. Controlling the Bane, especially that many, isn't a sure thing."

"I think you'll manage," she said coldly. Suddenly she made a signal with her hand and the boat growled back to life and started to crawl forward.

It was going to be pointless to fight them, that much was obvious.

So all I could do was start thinking *stay away*.

The massive boat pulled alongside the dock, and with jerky movements, the Bane along the shore started moving toward us.

One of them had been standing on the boardwalk and was moving at a quick rate. His legs moved at jerky intervals as if he were walking through tar.

"I suggest you make it stop," Margaret said, turning cold eyes on me. "Because if you can't do what your friend West said you could do, we have no reason to try and keep you alive."

"Just shoot it!" I yelled as I watched it make its way closer. It stumbled as its legs froze.

"Call this a test," she said.

By now the Bane had climbed to its feet again and was sprinting toward the dock.

"Stop!" I yelled, my heart pounding in my chest.

And it instantly froze in place.

"The water," I said, my voice shaking more than I would have liked. "Now."

It jumped off the dock. It hit the water with hissing sounds and a quick pop of light before it shorted out and sank out of sight.

I slowly met Margaret's eyes. That wicked grin was back. "Now that's more like it," she said. "Test completed. Shoot the rest of them."

The air was instantly alive with the sound of gunfire. Their bodies dropped on the shore.

"Let's move!" Alistar screamed.

The dolly I was chained to suddenly jerked to motion as one of the men grabbed the back of it and started pushing me out onto the dock. And everyone was running.

When we got to the end of the boardwalk and out onto a road, I saw why.

A good one hundred Bane were climbing out of buildings, running down roads. All called by the noise of their shots.

Stay back, I thought, over and over.

"Stay away from us!" I yelled.

More and more bodies climbed out of buildings.

My connection wasn't very strong with so many of them, but my captors fired as we ran. And I was able to keep them far enough away to keep any of them from touching us.

We had run for less than a minute when one of the armed men pulled open a heavy door in the sidewalk. A set of stairs dropped into the darkness. Someone grabbed the metal plate beneath my feet, and the two of them lifted me and down we dropped.

Once everyone had clambered inside, the door was closed and I heard a lock slide into place.

The lighting was dim and it took even my eyes a few moments to adjust.

We were in some kind of tunnel. Crumbling brick, stone, and wood walls stretched out before us. Moisture was heavy in the air. Everything tasted like mildew. Gas lamps hung every so often, providing little light to see by.

They carried me down the tunnel. As we moved, other's popped their heads out from doors. Each of them was as pale and sickly looking as the last.

I didn't have to ask questions. They survived in this city by never seeing the sun.

But that was only going to last so long. The Bane were Evolving past that need.

We entered a large room. The floor was dirty and dusty, just like all the walls and the crumbling ceiling.

The men carrying me set the dolly down and Margaret and Alistar stood before me.

"Welcome to the Underground," she said.

"I think I'll decline that welcome," I growled.

"Then decline it," she said, her expression going sour. "But you're not going anywhere."

"Why are you doing this?" I said. I wasn't sure if I felt any better when her armed men started disbanding from the room. "I mean, you're human. Aren't we supposed to be helping each other survive? Not kidnapping each other."

"Exactly!" she exploded. Her eyes blazed and she seemed to grow six inches. "Those of us who are left are supposed to help each other! Each of us has a duty to reclaim our world. But your people keep their technology to themselves. They let that weapon sit and rot on the roof when they could be using it to clear our country, our continent!"

"What did you expect?" I spat back. "You came in with secrets and lies and guns and just expected us to hand it over to you?"

"I expected you all to see what the right thing to do was," she said coldly as she took a step closer to me. "We are growing fewer and fewer each and every day. You want to know what the estimated percentage of the remaining human population is now? Less than half a percent! Ninety-nine point five percent of the population has been infected. If we don't do something *now*, we are handing the planet over to the Bane."

The last statistic I had heard was ninety-eight. And even though it had only changed by one and a half percent, it was crushing to hear it.

I didn't have anything to say in response.

"We're not done with your friends down south," Margaret said. She placed her hands on her hips and took another step closer. "But we have a new subject to learn from first."

"I'm not telling you anything until I see that West is safe." Everything in me screamed to find a way out of this place, to not say a word. But I couldn't just leave West here unaware of what these people were really doing.

"And I'm happy to oblige," she said with that repulsive smile. I realized then why it was so vile. Her teeth were a disgusting mix of yellow and brown and the ones on the left side of her mouth were horridly crooked. "Right this way."

Alistar came behind me and wheeled me down another tunnel.

"I seriously suggest you don't say a word, or even breathe," Margaret said as we slowed at the end of a tunnel. "He is never to know you are here."

"I understand," I said with a dead voice.

We stopped outside a door with a cloudy window. Alistar wheeled me right up to it.

West was seated inside, talking to a man with a bushy beard that didn't fit his narrow body. The man tapped the device in West's chest, speaking words I couldn't hear.

"Thank you," I said quietly and they started wheeling me down another tunnel. "What is this place?" I asked when we had some distance between us.

"The Underground of Seattle," Alistar said. So he did speak for himself after all. "The majority of the city of Seattle burned in the late 1800's. The ground level frequently flooded with the tides and rain though, so instead of rebuilding, they built on top of the remains. These tunnels are what's left of the original city. We've extended them into the basements of other buildings, securing them."

"How many of you are there?"

"That doesn't concern you," Margaret said in her cold voice. We reached another door which she pulled open and Alistar wheeled me into it.

I was unprepared for this room.

A single light bulb hung from the ceiling. In the middle of the small room, was a steel table.

It took everything I had in me not to start screaming for my release, not to break my cybernetic bones to get free.

The sound of a drill was echoing in my brain.

"Welcome to your room," Margaret said.

Alistar wheeled me to one corner and parked me there.

"It's been a long day," she said as they walked to the door. "We'll be back for you tomorrow morning. I hope you're comfortable."

They stepped outside and the door locked with a solid grinding sound of a metal post sliding into the wall.

And I was left there, chained to the dolly.

ELEVEN

I'd nearly tipped myself over in the struggle to free myself. The skin covering my ankles was torn and bleeding. I wore the flesh on my wrists away trying to escape my bonds. My cybernetic bones clanged against the chains.

But I'd gained no freedom.

Cyclones of emotions ripped through me. I'd been buoyed by rage and hatred for hours. I'd struggled against my bonds, my tiny new world washed in red.

But slowly uncertainty, bordering on fear, crept in.

What were they planning to do with me?

Assumptions were easy to make with that steel table in the middle of the room.

"She's afraid," a voice from the past echoed.

The drill screamed and the air was cold.

I closed my eyes, trying to force the dreams and memories out of my head.

"Doesn't she ever get tired?

"She's never been this aggressive before."

There was so much red. Metal and blood.

My breath caught in my chest and I jerked my arms again, tearing my flesh more.

Subject is again devoid of emotion.

"Sometimes they would let us play together."

"Damn it, West," I hissed, my eyes sliding open and rising to the damp looking ceiling. "What did you do?"

I'd probably only been this room for a few hours, and already I was losing my mind.

But I'd been losing my mind before these people had cyborgnapped me. Avian had been right, it was only a matter of time before I would have snapped. And who knows who I would have broken with me.

I knew the answer to that question. I'd already started doing it.

West.

Despite how beyond angry I was with him in that moment, I hoped wherever he was, he was safe. As safe as he could be.

I assumed he would be. He'd left home willingly in order to escape me.

But how safe was everyone in New Eden now? How much damage had been done before my captors left?

A horrifying thought occurred to me then. What if they hadn't all left? How did I know that they had all returned to Seattle?

How did I know that I was the only hostage?

"Avian." His name whispered over my lips with the skip of a heartbeat and ice in my stomach.

No, he'd been fighting when I went down. I saw that. I had to tell myself that he was fine, back in New Eden.

These people wanted to study me. Avian was normal, human. They would gain nothing by taking him.

But Avian tended to do stupid, irrational things when it came to my safety. What would he do when he found I was gone?

A low growl worked its way up my chest.

I'd kill every single one of them if anything happened to him.

I counted the seconds eagerly.

Sometime they were going to have to release me. Sometime these chains were going to loosen. Sometime someone was going to accidently grant me a tiny window of opportunity and I would exploit it.

I was going to make it out of here.

And I was going to make it home.

I waited in the pitch black, in the musty dark. I plotted all the ways I was going to choke Alistar. The way I would break in all of Margaret's disgusting teeth.

And finally, the dim bulb above my head flickered back on.

Feet shuffled out in the hall. Muffled voices tricked in through the cracks around the door.

The knob turned, and the door shrieked as it was pushed open.

A tiny man with thick, black glasses stepped timidly into the room. His small shoulders were covered with a white lab coat. His shoes were ragged and worn. He wouldn't make eye contact as I stared at him with dark eyes.

He carried a device with him. It reminded me of a radio but had something that looked like a tiny computer hooked to it.

"You are holding me prisoner here," I said through clenched teeth. "We are both human, we do not treat each other like this. Not since the world started teetering on the edge of extinction."

"That's apparently debatable," he said. His voice as small and weak sounding as his physique.

"What?" I questioned, not sure I had even heard what he had said.

"Us both being human." He pushed a button on the radio looking portion of the device. It started making scratchy sounds.

"You don't know anything about me," I said, shaking my head, flexing my muscles, straining against my bonds. If only I could break free. I could snap this tiny man with little effort.

"You're emitting a low frequency signal," he said, turning the device so I could see it. A screen showed two barely twitching brilliant green lines. "Two, actually. One that is similar to the what the Bane emit. It doesn't really do anything. It's more a side effect of all of their cybernetic components. But the other, I'm not really sure what it is. Fascinating."

"I swear to you, if you don't let me go I will call a hoard of Bane down here to destroy every living soul in this hovel!" I screamed. And suddenly the idea, however startling it was, seemed like an option to gain my freedom.

"I don't suggest it," he said, his eyes dropping to my feet. "You see, while you were drugged, we attached a live electrical wire to that lovely thing you're chained to. I just have to push this little button if you do anything I don't like, and a shock strong enough to all but kill you will run through your mechanical body."

"You son of a—"

"Language, please," he said, his voice rising just slightly for the first time.

I bit the inside of my cheek to keep from spewing more vile things. My insides were full of them.

"Now," he said, pulling a stool from beneath the table. It scraped the concrete floor and the sound echoed off the stone walls. "I have some questions. If you don't mind."

"Doesn't seem I have much of a choice," I said, my voice low.

"Not really," he said, his eyes meeting mine. They were dead eyes, gray and hollow. They reminded me of the eyes of the Bane. "We'll get our answers one way or another."

"I don't intend to do this the easy way."

"That's fine," he said. His voice was madly calm and even. Almost as if he was talking to an animal he didn't wish to scare away. "But for your safety, I suggest you change your mind on that."

He didn't wait for me to respond and placed another device on the table. It was an old fashioned tape recorder. The tape started slowly spinning when he pushed the button with the red circle.

"How long were you at NovaTor Biotics?" he asked, his eyes meeting mine again.

"How do you know I was ever there?" I said, once again trying to gain any wiggle room in my chains.

"Your friend accidently shared quite a few secrets," he said.

"What did he tell you?"

"Not as much as we would like to know," he said. "That is why I am asking you these questions. Now, how long were you at NovaTor?"

I held his eyes for a long time. There was something terrifying about this little man. Like he knew how to twist things into the shape he wanted to see, break you in ways you didn't know you could be broken.

This little man was a wolf in sheep's clothing.

And maybe, just maybe, if I cooperated, I'd make it out of here alive to get back to Avian and New Eden.

"I was born there," I said, my voice almost too quiet to hear at first. "My mother worked at NovaTor."

"Thank you," he said with the barest hint of a smile forming on his face. "And when were you given TorBane?"

"As an infant," I said, recalling the truths Dr. Beeson had revealed. "I was underdeveloped, born premature. I would have died without it."

"And you were the first?" he asked. "The first human to be given TorBane."

"Yes."

"And how is it that you don't spread TorBane like all the others?"

"I don't know," I said, my voice rising with my frustration.

"What do you mean, you don't know?" For the first time, there was a hint of impatience in his voice.

And I finally knew what they were really after.

"I'm saying that I don't know why I don't spread the infection," I said, my emotional hurricane calming. It's easier to form a plan when you know what it is your enemies want. "I don't understand everything that was done to me. I know it has something to do with my young age and controlled dosages. But it isn't as if I've had notes to study."

He just looked at me for a moment after that. Normally with a silence like that, after hearing information like he just had, you can tell they are formulating a theory or a plan, or something.

But his eyes just looked impassive.

"Thank you for your cooperation," he suddenly said. He'd been so quiet and still that I nearly jumped when he finally seemed to come back to life. "We will let you know if we wish to ask you more questions." And he stood to leave.

"Wait, that's it?" I said, my eyes following him as he pulled the door open. "That was all you wanted to know?"

"For now," he said, and closed the door behind him.

By my rough calculations, they left me there in that room for another twenty-four hours.

It left me with far too much time to think.

There was that question he had asked.

Why didn't I infect others? How did TorBane exist in me, as it was designed to, when it just took everyone else over?

I'd told him the truth when I told him I didn't really know.

Dr. Beeson had told me once but he didn't exactly spell it out. I didn't understand the science. I understood that TorBane worked on me the way it was intended to work on the rest of the world.

I wasn't going to be able to give them the answers they wanted.

My head jerked up when the ground beneath my feet shook and even in my isolated cell, I could hear shouting and gun fire.

I jerked against my bonds once more, my bones clanging against the chains. The skin around my wounds was swollen and red, attempting to heal.

The sound of gunfire drew closer, the shouts grew more desperate. Screams ricochet off the walls.

And suddenly the firing stopped and the voices grew calmer.

I hated this blindness. I hated being bound. I hated everything about Seattle.

What was happening?

The door to my cell screamed as it was pushed open and two guards appeared in the doorway. They didn't look at me though. They dragged something behind them, keeping their heads down as they pulled.

When they cleared the doorway, I saw what it was.

They each grasped a metal hook. The other end sank into the chest of a Bane.

"Did it touch anyone?" I couldn't help but asking. "How'd it get in?"

But they didn't answer me. They dragged the bullet riddled carcass into the opposite corner and left the body in a heap. The two of them then turned and left, locking the door behind them.

Great, not only was I locked up, but I now had a rotting mechanical corpse as a cell mate.

I studied its form where it lay on the ground as the noise outside the door died away. It was a female. She looked like she was probably the same age as me. Her stark pale skin was a heavy contrast to the metallic eyes that stared emptily up at the ceiling. Most of the left side of her jaw was a mangled mess of muscle and metal and blood. Her chest was the same way.

I then noticed the simple band that encircled her left ring finger.

She'd been engaged or married at some point. She'd loved someone and committed to spend the rest of her life with them.

But then TorBane got her and she unknowingly made another kind of lifetime commitment.

The sense of helplessness I had once felt back in the mountains of Eden crept back in on me. We'd managed to wipe out millions of Bane in Los Angeles, but there were still billions left out there. The numbers were staggering.

Would we just keep fighting to the very last human? Would we keep running and hiding in our holes in the ground until that last person sat alone in the dark, with the weight of an annihilated race on their shoulders?

I felt sorry for that last person. And I prayed it would never be me.

⋘━━━

Eight more hours by my guess. That's how long I sat alone with that body.

Then the door opened again, the same two guards came back in with their hooks, and dragged the body out. It was just me again.

I could only assume they had been waiting for dark to get rid of the body. They had placed it with the one person who couldn't be infected until that time came.

With the body gone, my head started to sag, and my eyelids fluttered. Exhaustion was finally overtaking me. I'd made myself stay awake the entire time I'd been in the Underground. I'd had no food or water. I was part Bane, but enough of me was human to be weakened.

There was no doubt in my mind they were depriving me on purpose. I couldn't fight back if I was too weak to keep my eyelids open.

I had frantic dreams. Dreams of fighting the Bane in the forest surrounding old Eden. Dreams of watching West's eyes change from human white to metallic Bane. Dreams of Avian being choked to death by a mechanical Margaret.

"Rise and shine."

My head jerked up, my eyes struggling to focus for a moment.

Speak of the devil.

Margaret stood across the table from me, her hands resting on it, her gaze fixed on me.

"I hope you rested well," she said, her eyes dancing.

"Best sleep of my life," I growled.

That disgusting grin of hers spread and she chuckled. "You really should stop struggling you know. That looks like it hurts." She indicated my wrists and ankles. "But that's right. You don't feel pain."

I just continued to glare at her.

"It is indeed rather convenient your friend doesn't know you're here. He's quite willing to talk to Tara about you when he thinks you're back home safe with your lover."

Her words stung. Far more than I wanted them to.

"He explained how you don't feel things like pain. How you didn't used to feel much of any emotion," her eyes darkened in a way I didn't understand. "He told me how you were the first. That if it wasn't for your early arrival into this world, and for your fragile state, TorBane might not have ever been developed."

And I started to understand her hatred and hostility toward me. She was starting to uncover my past and how I helped to bring about the end of the world.

There was something personal about this behind those eyes.

She'd lost someone. Someone more important to her than just the rest of the world.

"But I think maybe," she said, her voice dropping an octave. "Just maybe, you can help save it."

"If you know a way, trust me, I'm all ears," I said. My stomach felt heavy and sea-sick like.

"Thank you for your cooperation. I am glad to hear that you are willing to help," she said, that deadly smile returning. "Bring them in!"

The door suddenly opened and five new bodies filled the small room. Two guards, two men in white lab coats, and another woman in scrubs.

"What are you doing?" I said, the urgency in my voice rising. "Wait! I said I would help you!"

"And you are going to help us," Margaret said as the guards lifted me with the dolly. While they did so, one of the men in the lab coats sank a needle into my neck. The world instantly grew hazy. "But unfortunately you can't *tell* us what we need to see."

TWELVE

The man sat in front of me, turned to the side so he was facing that flat rectangle. His fingers flashed over the pad that sat on the table, each of his fingers rapidly tapping certain points on it.

I watched him as he worked, observing the details that made up the whole that was him. His hair was so dark. So much darker than my own. It was longer than many of the other men I knew. It curled slightly at the ends.

His skin was dark as well and almost looked black in the creases and wrinkles. He didn't have as many of those as Dr. Evans did though. Dr. Beeson was much younger.

I felt differently toward Dr. Beeson than I did toward Dr. Evans.

But I didn't know how to identify that feeling.

I'd been taught to observe others and identify their body language. Shifting eyes and skittish hands indicated nervousness. A smile and bright eyes usually meant happiness. Tears and trembling lips were surely sadness.

But when it came to what happened inside of me, there wasn't anything.

I'd stared at myself in a mirror for exactly ten minutes once. My face had been blank. No body language to read. I'd tried smiling like I'd seen others do. I tried frowning. But it didn't look right.

I realized then that there had to be something going on inside to make the outside look correct.

My inside was mostly hollow.

"How do you feel, Eve?" Dr. Beeson asked, finally turning toward me. His eyes looked sad.

"I feel like myself," I said.

He studied me, much like I had studied him moments ago.

"You don't feel angry?" he asked. "You don't feel sad?"

I shook my head.

He kept looking at me, not saying anything.

So I kept looking back at him.

His eyes rose to look at someone behind me. "The last adjustment is holding. She doesn't need another."

"Very good," a voice said. I turned in my seat to find the speaker. There was a large television with a gruff-looking man on the screen. His eyes narrowed at me. "Keep us updated."

"Yes, sir," Dr. Beeson said. I turned back to him, and noticed uncertainty in his eyes.

Dr. Beeson didn't like the man on the screen.

"Try it again," the woman said patiently. "Look at the letters. Sound them out."

I looked from her face back to the book. The words seemed to shift and rearrange themselves on the page. But I narrowed my eyes, focusing on one word.

"Bio..." I struggled to make them stay focused. "Bio...log...ical."

"Very good," she said, a smile spreading on her face. She patted my back. "Read on."

"The biological reasons for this are unknown. Possible exp...lanations include increased risk of pregnancy complications." I paused, looking from the article to the woman again. "Why am I reading this?"

"Because it helps you learn," she said, her eyes meeting mine. Something changed in them, but I didn't know how to recognize it.

I blinked twice at her before turning back to the article.

I was almost finished reading it when Dr. Evans stepped inside the room. I met his eyes and he gave me a sad smile. His smile was always sad.

"Keep reading," the woman said. "I'll be with you in a moment."

I kept reading.

The woman and Dr. Evans slipped to the back of the room and talked in quiet voices.

"Any sign that the dyslexia is improving?" Dr. Evans asked.

"Slowly but surely," she said.

I tried to keep my reading smooth and even so they would not be able to tell I was listening.

"This is taking longer than we expected," he said. "Subject one has recovered much more quickly and from a much more serious neurological condition."

The woman was quiet for a moment. "I wish you wouldn't call them that. We could give them real names."

Dr. Evans paused, the air serious, even from across the room. "It's easier this way."

Neither of them said anything and finally I heard the door open and then click shut again.

"This is argued to be caused by an unbalanced gen..." I struggled.

"Genomic." The woman was flustered and distracted if she was giving me the full word without making me sound it out.

"Genomic imprinting," I continued. "Favoring paternal genes in the case of autism and maternal genes in the case of psychosis."

"Very good," the woman said. "You can take a break before you are taken to the gym."

And she turned and left.

Since I didn't normally feel pain, I didn't know how to describe the feeling.

Like cold and sandpaper squeezing all the nerves in my head.

It wasn't crushing or like fire, like some of the pain I had experienced before.

This was like slow suffocation.

My eyelids fluttered open for a moment. There was no detail to the space around me, just hazy gray.

"…can't go out like this," a voice said. "Look at her."

"I don't see how we have much of a choice."

Goosebumps prickled along my skin. The air around me was chilly and moist.

That cold, grating feeling in my head pulsed once and darkness started rising in my eyes.

An alarm was sounding and I placed my hands over my ears in attempt to block it out. People dashed down the halls, shouting, fear in their eyes.

Dr. Evans peered around the corner, looking both ways down the hall, before turning back to me.

"We're going to run for Dr. Beeson's office, okay?" he said. He was just as scared as everyone else. "You're not going to say a word and you're going to do whatever he tells you. Don't say anything, got it?"

I nodded, my eyes wide.

There was something clawing under my skin, fighting to break out.

I suddenly hoped Dr. Beeson might do an adjustment and make the feeling go away.

"Let's go!" he yelled.

My hand gripped tightly in his, we sprinted down the hall.

THIRTEEN

"We can't afford to wait any longer."

I knew that voice and it made my fists ball.

"You rouse her too quickly and we could lose her," a voice said.

And suddenly everything in me flooded back to life.

I was off the table in a frantic scramble. Finding Margaret at my side, my right hand closed around her throat. Grabbing a shining blade from the table, I backed her into a corner and held the blade to her throat.

"Let me go," I hissed.

There were three others in the room. A man who looked like he must be a doctor, and two soldiers.

"Calm down, Eve," the doctor said. "Or you're going to make yourself bleed to death."

As he spoke I felt a wet, warm trickle work its way down my neck. I glanced down just a moment too long.

One guard snatched Margaret out of my grip, but not without the blade nicking her jawline. She cursed loudly. The other guard rushed me, pressing his shotgun across my throat, pinning me to the wall.

It had been a line of blood that had distracted me, running from the back of my head, down around my throat and in between my breasts.

"Please calm down," the doctor said, wild fear in his eyes. He held his hands up as if he were surrendering. "You're already tearing the stitches."

"What are you doing to me?" I barely managed to get the words out. My body shook with rage and uncertainty.

"Gaining knowledge," Margaret said with a growl. "Look, there isn't much time. As much as it pains me to say it, we need your help."

"Haven't I already been helping you?" I spat back.

"Could you just shut up for a moment?!" she bellowed, crossing the room and getting in my face.

My mouth closed and I stared back at her.

"Alistar and his team went out for supplies last night and have gotten themselves trapped in a building. The Bane weren't supposed to be awake."

"You know that rule is quickly dying, right?" I said as the guard stepped away, releasing my throat. "That only applies to a few of them now. The older the Hunter, the more they're awake."

Something passed over her eyes that told me she had only recently discovered this.

"It's because of the clouds here, isn't it?" I said as the pieces started to fall into place. "It's delayed their Evolution. They're only just now starting to be active at night, aren't they?"

It took her a moment to respond. "Yes."

"They've been waking up at night everywhere else I've been for months now." I recalled the first time we'd learned that lesson. We'd lost Tye that night, a good soldier, and Avian's best friend and cousin.

"We weren't expecting it," she said, her voice weak sounding for the first time since I had met her. "And now one of our teams is trapped inside a building. We need you to go and get them out."

"Why would I ever help you?" I hissed.

"Because West's surgery is scheduled for tomorrow and I swear on my mother's grave we will let him Evolve if you don't do as we say."

My insides swelled, filling with hot ash and burning coals. I wanted to snap her neck and continue breaking every bone in her body. Rage was becoming a part of who I was lately. I was a caged animal and I'd been backed into a corner.

"What time of day is it right now?" I asked.

"It's ten in the morning."

"And you want me to go out there right now?" I demanded. I couldn't help it as my hands rose and I shoved her away from me. She wasn't expecting it and tripped backwards into the arms of the soldier who had pulled her away from me.

"If we wait any longer their location will be breached," she shouted back, righting herself, once again getting in my face.

"They will pull me apart, limb from limb this time of day."

"It's raining heavily," she said. Her eyes told me she knew this was a poor defense. "They're less active when it rains. Some of them are too Evolved to go out in the rain without being shorted out. You stand a better chance. And we'll send a soldier with you."

I just kept her eyes for a long moment and finally shook my head.

"I want to see West again," I said. Something in my body sagged, knowing I had no choice but to bend to this woman's will.

She took a second to answer. "Give us a minute."

And then she and the doctor left, leaving me with the guards.

I couldn't help it as my hands rose to my head. At the crown of my head, there was a three inch circle of hair that I found shaven away. It was sticky with blood and my fingers ran over careful stitches.

It was more horrifying than it should have been.

Finding a hair tie still around my wrist, I carefully pulled my hair back into a ponytail, hiding the bald spot.

My hands came out streaked with sticky blood.

"This way," Margaret said, opening the door again and nodding down the hall with her head.

The guards stepped behind me, pointing their guns at my back as we walked. We snaked through a maze of crumbling passages, passing doors and openings into other rooms. We stopped at a wall with a glass window.

"Don't let him see you," Margaret warned again.

"I won't," I said as I carefully peered around the window through the dark.

111

West sat on a grubby, broken-down couch. He looked relaxed, leaning back, his ankle crossed over the other knee. A smile broke out over his face and he laughed. He was talking to Tara. She laughed back, a dimple forming in her right cheek. There were others in the room too, eating small meals, talking quickly and nervously. This must have been some sort of a mess hall.

"He's fine," Margaret said, placing a hand on my arm and pulling me away gently.

"I need a shotgun, a handgun and a few grenades if you've got them," I said.

I swore under my breath as I stared up at the metal hatch above my head.

My head was pounding. It must have been really bad if I could actually feel it through my chips pain blockers.

My legs were wobbling and I could tell I'd lost more blood that was safe to go out running about a Bane-infested city.

During the day.

"You ready for this?" I asked. I looked back.

The man behind me nodded his head. In many ways he reminded me of Avian, with his closely shaved hair and lean frame. But he was younger than Avian, probably closer to West's age. I'd guess twenty.

He carried not one, but three shotguns and one assault rifle. He had probably eight grenades attached to the utility belt around his waist.

"What's your name?" I asked.

"Why?" he questioned.

"Because if we die today, I want to know the name of the man I'm going down with."

This might have rattled a lot of people. Even a lot of soldiers. But there was a darkness behind his eyes that seemed to understand.

"Tristan," he said.

"Let's go, Tristan."

Gripping the lock of the hatch, I twisted it and pushed it open.

My arm was instantly soaked as the rain started falling into the hole. Checking to make sure the road was clear, I climbed out of the hole and onto the sidewalk. Tristan followed me an instant later and closed the hatch again.

"This way," he said, pointing with his rifle up a street, away from the water.

The roads rose quickly the further we went from the water. The rain ran down the gutters furiously, creating a small river. My hair instantly stuck to my face, washing the blood from my face and neck.

We hugged buildings as we ran up the road. But I cringed every time I looked inside a storefront and saw the Bane, standing there, staring emptily out at us.

"You know they're not going to stay like that for long, right?" I said as we crouched behind a car. "The Sleepers are going to wake up."

"That's what we've been theorizing," he said. "That's why Margaret's gotten so crazy. She's desperate."

We dashed across the road and hugged the building again as we worked our way up the street.

"You mean she wasn't always this...hostile?" I said, keeping my voice low.

"She's always been a little intense, but you have to understand, you being here, TorBane, it's all personal," he said as his eyes swept the buildings around us.

"What do you mean?" I asked, scanning the roofline across the street.

"Margaret had two daughters. The oldest one, Bridget, she was fifteen when she was infected last year. There was a breach," he said. We both saw movement at the same time and ducked behind a car. I peeked through a window and watched a boy cross the street. He still looked human except for his bare, mechanical feet.

"But she also had a three year old who was dying of liver failure before the Evolution," Tristan whispered. "No organ donors came up, no transplant came available. Margaret sold everything to pay for her to get a TorBane upgrade."

I'd seen the evidence of everyone who had turned, who had been infected. But it was always so much worse hearing stories about the first generation, who embraced TorBane without knowing what it would shortly do to them and the rest of the world.

"So you understand why Margaret hates you so much," he said, his eyes meeting mine. They were green.

"I can't blame her," I said. "I hate myself too sometimes."

"Sounds to me like it wasn't your fault," he said, his voice more understanding than I deserved.

"Road's clear again," I said, looking out the window.

We bolted down the road as the rain continued to fall.

I couldn't help the instinct to fire when I heard the clatter to my left.

A Bane hurtled itself at a window when it saw us moving. I fired in its direction, shattering the large glass window and took it out. But there were a dozen others standing next to it, staring out at us, their muscles, or whatever they still had flexing and twitching to jump out after us. This group was almost one hundred percent mechanical-looking. Most of them didn't even have skin anymore.

But they stood frozen just under the cover of the building.

"The rain," I said in awe. "They won't come out because of the rain!"

"Let's move!" Tristan shouted.

We sprinted, turning down another road.

Glass continually shattered as we moved, Bane throwing themselves out at us, only to twitch and short out as the rain crept into their mechanical innards. They could only stand under the cover of buildings and race along after us or die.

"How much further?" I asked. I was heavily weighed down with ammunition, but the amount of bullets I had didn't equal the number of Bane that were surrounding us.

"Two more blocks," Tristan called.

With all the adrenaline pumping through my system, I hadn't realized my head had stopped pounding and the wound was no longer bleeding. TorBane was healing my body.

Tristan turned down another block. As soon as we rounded the corner, he turned, grabbed two of the grenades from his belt, pulled the pins, and tossed them at the hoard that chased after us.

Body parts littered the street. And there was a horrible grinding, crunching sound as the side of the building broke apart and crashed to the street, crushing the bodies, and narrowly missing us.

"Good aim," I said, my pace slowing slightly, now that the danger level had dropped a bit. My head was no longer pounding, but my legs were wobbly still and I felt slightly woozy.

"You okay?" he asked, turning concerned eyes on me.

"I can understand why that woman hates me, but damn her for making me less than what I should be and throwing me out to the Bane," I growled, my step faltering slightly.

"I don't know what they're doing to you," he said as we slowed to a walk. He pulled me behind a car and eased me down to the ground. "But I'm pretty sure there has to be a better method."

I wasn't sure what to say to him. I didn't know how much he knew about me or what they were trying to get from me.

"Desperate times make people act desperate," he said as his eyes met mine for a moment. "Desperation has a way of bringing out the worst in people."

"Yeah," was all I could say. Because I'd seen it too often. I'd seen it in myself on more than one occasion.

"You ready to go again?" he asked.

"Where are we actually headed anyway?" I asked. My head was slowly evening out.

"Our group was getting supplies at a hardware store when something went wrong. We're not entirely sure what happened," he said. "But they knew something was coming and they barricaded themselves in the bank across the street. There's a vault they're hiding in."

"Alistar is more than some soldier to Margaret, isn't he?" I asked, climbing to my feet. We started down the road again.

"He's her lover," Tristan said, shaking his head. "I don't get it. Margaret is... Margaret. How can he stand her?"

"Maybe he enjoys power-hungry women," I said, disgust rising in my stomach.

To my surprise, Tristan laughed. It was a deep, belly laugh. It was so unexpected, I couldn't help but smile too.

"That's it right there," he said, once again serious. Tristan pointed to a building sandwiched between a dozen others. Its front was stark marble white with gold trim. On the ground level, the entire front was nearly all glass.

"I know you're supposed to be able to communicate with them or something, but I think our best bet is to just fire as many rounds as we can," Tristan said.

"Sounds good to me," I said. "I can do my best to keep them away from us."

Tristan looked at me, his brows knitting together. "It doesn't really matter to me what you are," he said, his eyes trailing over me. "But so far I think you're pretty impressive."

117

"I'm also involved," I blurted.

A coy grin cracked on his lips. "That wasn't what I meant, but good to know. I'm just saying you're one impressive soldier."

My face turned warm with embarrassment. "Thanks," I muttered. "Let's go."

We jogged toward the building. I slowed as we approached the bank, stopping just out of sight.

There were seven of them inside. Advanced looking. Most of them had no flesh at all anymore.

Five of them stood in a line facing what must have been the vault. They were perfectly still, frozen like they were statues. One of them stood next to the combination, its hand pressed flat against the steel wall. And another had its hand on the dial, slowly rotating it to the right.

"What are they doing?" Tristan barely whispered.

The realization hit me just as the one turning the dial stopped turning it and I barely registered the faint click.

I started firing the same time the Bane yanked the vault open. Screams filled the air and metal scraped against marble as the Bane rushed into the vault.

"NO!" Tristan bellowed as he fired into the bank.

I didn't stop shooting. But I knew it was too late. The Bane were all over the five people inside.

"We've got to get out of here!" I screamed, grabbing the back of Tristan's soaked jacket and pulling him quickly back toward the doors.

The Bane then registered we were there.

Knowing they had completed their only reason for being—infecting humans—they turned and sprinted after us.

Tristan and I crashed to the road as we backed out of the bank, landing in a puddle. I kept firing, hitting two of the mechanical creatures that sprinted across the bank after us. They dropped in a heap.

But three others barreled right out of the building into the rain.

Hissing filled the air as two of them instantly shorted out and dropped to the ground as Tristan and I scrambled backwards. But the last one with more flesh than the others kept rushing forward.

Slipping in the rain, I lost my footing and was taken down just a moment too long.

The Bane was on top of me, its hands around my throat. My head was forced into a puddle. Water lapped just over my eyes, making my vision wave under the water.

It jerked over and over again as Tristan fired at it, but it didn't go down.

That familiar red rage flooded my system again and I wanted with everything in my system for this creature trying to kill me to meet a horrible end.

I watched as its hands left my throat and went to its own head. In one movement, it twisted its head violently to the left and up.

The head was ripped clean from its body.

It collapsed to the left of me with a splash that sent currents of electricity through the water to shock me endlessly.

A screamed leapt from my lips and then there were strong hands dragging me out of the puddle. Tristan swore, stumbling under my weight and stopping in the middle of the road.

"You've got to do it now," I faintly heard a voice. My system recovering from the electrocution, I stood and my vision cleared. The two Bane who were left stood just under the cover of the bank's opening, staring at Tristan and I. They wouldn't come out after us into the rain.

But next to them stood four people, and I saw Alistar's body lying on the floor behind them. He'd been mauled to death.

It was strange, seeing the Bane stand next to the four humans. But their only task in life was completed. They had no reason to pay them anymore attention.

"We're as good as dead," a woman said. "End us now before we end anyone else."

There was terror in the other three's eyes, but they each slowly nodded.

"I can't," Tristan said. His voice cracked.

"You have to," I said quietly, thinking of Tye.

Tristan's eyes fell to the ground and he wiped the back of his hand across his nose. He shook his head, swearing under his breath again.

"Will you help me?" he said, his eyes rising to meet mine.

It took me a moment to nod.

Tristan took four steps closer to the bank, his shotgun held loosely in his hand.

"I'm so sorry," he said, his voice rough and scratchy. "You've made it this long."

"No need for speeches," the woman said, tears streaming down her face. "Just get it over with, please."

Tristan nodded and waved me forward. I held my shotgun ready.

"You take the two on the right," he said to me. "I'll take the two on the left."

A lump formed in my throat as I raised my shotgun, leveling it on a very terrified looking man who had to be in his sixties. I was glad Tristan hadn't told me their names.

"Fire!" Tristan shouted.

And for the first time, I shot at a man who was still mostly human.

He dropped to the ground at the same time another woman did. The others screamed.

I couldn't wait for Tristan's command. I shot the woman who had spoken for them.

Apparently Tristan couldn't give the command again, because he fired at the same time I did.

We both stood frozen for a moment, Tristan with his shotgun still leveled. I was fairly sure he wasn't breathing.

"Let's go," I said, swallowing the lump in my throat.

The rain continued to fall harder and harder as we made our way back. Plenty of Bane had woken and watched us from the cover of the buildings. But as long as we stayed in the middle of the road, far from their reach, they left us alone.

I froze outside the hatch, unable to make myself go back down into that hole.

"Is she going to kill me?" I asked. "Since we failed?"

"I don't think so," Tristan said, clearing his throat. He had been trying hard the entire journey home to control his emotions. "You seem to be pretty valuable."

"Margaret has a short temper," I said hollowly.

His green eyes met mine. "I won't let her do anything to you."

"Somehow I don't think you can stop her from getting whatever it is she wants from me."

"That doesn't mean I can't try," he said, his grip tightening on his shotgun.

"Why are you here, Tristan?" I asked, my eyes narrowing at him. "You don't seem to fit in with this crowd."

He shrugged. "What else am I supposed to do? It's safer to stay in groups. I'd never last out there on my own. We've got to stick together."

I looked at him for a long time. Maybe it was all about uncontrollable fate. You had to live with the people you could find these days. West had first been with a harsh military group, and then a group that was only a step above marauders.

But I'd found Eden. A place where people were good, where people did their best to help one another.

Tristan had crazy Margaret.

My fate was better than his.

And even though I had only known him for an hour, I wanted to save him from his fate. But I was powerless to do so.

"Are they really going to help my friend?" I asked.

Tristan broke eye contact and gave a sniff before wiping the rain water from his nose with the back of his hand. "Margaret will keep her word. She's insane, but she'll do what she says."

"Will you make sure?" I asked. "That she helps him? If I can't do it myself?"

He met my eyes again for a long time and finally nodded.

"Thank you."

"Ready?"

"No," I answered honestly.

There was sympathy in his eyes, but what was he supposed to do?

He bent and unlocked the hatch and held it open for me.

FOURTEEN

I didn't even see Margaret.

As soon as Tristan and I entered the tunnel we were greeted by four guards. Tristan explained what happened and I was instantly bound.

Tristan held my eyes as they started dragging me away.

"I'll make sure," he had said. "I promise."

And so I went willingly with the guards back to my room.

The doctors were waiting for me.

Sometimes there was darkness. Heavy and warm and light and cold.

Sometimes there was a fuzzy gray ceiling and voices in the haze that I couldn't see.

But most of the time there was a kaleidoscope of broken memories and nightmares.

"Would you like a balloon?" the man asked as he crouched in front of me. He had a lot of hair above his lip, but the rest of his face was smooth.

"Do you have a red one?" I asked. I sat on my bed, my legs tucked into my chest.

"I think I do," he said, his voice excited and kind. He dug into the pocket of his white jacket, and produced a floppy red balloon. He pulled something black out of his other pocket and blew up the balloon with it. It filled, long and skinny.

He then twisted it in different sections, the rubber squeaking high pitched as he did.

"It's a dog!" I said excitedly as I recognized the form.

"That's right," he said with a laugh and a smile. "Here you go."

He handed it to me and I took it, absolutely delighted.

"Are you ready for your test?" he asked.

"I don't like the tests," I said, my eyes growing dark and shaking my head.

"I know," he said, his tone understanding. "But we need to make sure your heart is working like it should. I'll make you a deal. If you're really good and do the test, I'll make you a horse when we're done."

"Promise?" I asked.

"Promise."

"How about this one instead?" he asked, holding up the green marker.

"No," I said, gritting my teeth. "I want the blue one."

"But I need the blue one," he said, his tone rising.

"I had it first!" I yelled.

"No you didn't!"

"Yes, I did!" I screamed, reaching for the blue marker. He gripped it tightly and I tugged, only to fall backward when the cap came off and I lost my balance.

He laughed at me.

"I hate you, West!" I screamed, throwing the cap at him. To my satisfaction, it hit him right in the eye and he immediately started crying.

"Dad!" he wailed.

Dr. Evans Jr. was instantly in the room, the crying West wrapped around his legs.

"Really, Eve?" he chided me. "We don't throw things. And hate isn't a kind word."

"But I hate him," I growled, scowling at West who glowered right back at me. "He doesn't share!"

"West?" Dr. Evans questioned, looking down at West.

"She started it!" he shouted, glaring back at me.

"Okay," Dr. Evans said. "I think that's enough for one day."

West stuck his tongue out at me as his father led him out of the room.

I stuck mine right back out at him.

They all stared at me.

There were four of them with Dr. Evans, and they all looked at me.

"She's perfectly healthy now?" one of them asked. "No complications?"

Dr. Evans shook his head. "Her heart was only developed to eighty percent of what it should have been, her lungs only to sixty. But they both function perfectly now."

"And the other one?" another man asked.

"Her development is slower," Dr. Evans said. His voice sounded tired and heavy. "We weren't sure how TorBane would react with a psychological disorder so this is totally uncharted territory. But she's coming along. She's talking, she's well behaved the majority of the time. She's slowly learning how to interact."

"Tell us about the regenerative abilities."

Dr. Evans eyes met mine and something in them lightened.

"Eve," he said kindly. "Would you come over here for a moment?"

I got to my feet, my eyes meeting the strangers warily. I crossed the room and gripped Dr. Evans' jacket tightly in one fist.

"Can you show me that cut you got the other day?" he asked me.

I held up my left hand, exposing my palm.

"The nurse dropped a glass two days ago and it shattered on the floor in Eve two's bedroom. Eve here tried to help clean it up and cut herself. But as you can see, it's completely healed."

This brought a smile to the strangers' faces. "Perfect," one woman said.

"I think TorBane and chip X731 are going to be a perfect match, Dr. Evans."

"No!" I screamed as I leapt across my bed. I grabbed my hair brush and threw it at the man. "Don't touch me!"

"Come back here, you little..." He chased after me.

I wrapped my tiny hand around the neck of my lamp and hurled it at him next. It caught him in the shoulder and shattered.

A growl ripped from his throat and he tackled me to the ground.

A sharp pain pricked in my neck as he jabbed a needle into my skin.

Everything seemed to slow instantly.

I jabbed my finger into his eye and he reeled backwards into a wall.

"Don't..." I tried to yell but my throat felt thick. "Don't touch me."

"Eve," a familiar voice said. Dr. Evans. The younger one. "Everything is going to be alright."

"No", I shook my head. I tried to press my back further into the corner. My vision blurred and the dark shadows before me blended together.

"She's never been this aggressive before," a voice said. It felt like someone was screaming into my ear. Everything was too loud. I pressed my hands over the sides of my head, trying to block it all out.

"She's afraid," a lighter voice said.

I couldn't make out any details anymore as I opened and closed my eyes, trying to clear my vision. My head felt fuzzy and clouded.

There was a pair of warm arms underneath me and I could feel them moving.

My vision was totally black by now and at some point, someone slid my eyelids closed when I couldn't do it myself.

They changed my clothes and there was a strange buzzing sound.

Soon my head felt lighter and cold.

The next second all I could make out was the scent of steel under me. There were voices in the dark, talking excitedly behind me.

Then there was the sound of a drill.

"What's wrong with her?"

West sat in front of me, building a tower with foam blocks. But he kept looking up at me.

"She had her surgery," a woman said. I looked over at her and blinked. She looked at me. There was something about her face that looked off. Her brows were pulled together slightly. A sheen of sweat beaded on her forehead. There was a bit of moisture under her arms.

"Are you scared of her?" West asked, looking at the woman too.

She looked at West, but then her eyes fell quickly to the floor. "Build your tower," she said.

West stacked another block, then looked up at me again.

"She normally tries to take my stuff," he said, still looking at me. "Why is she just sitting there?"

"Build your tower," the woman said again. "Don't worry about it."

"The other one is the same way," West said, turning back to his blocks. He made a fence around his tower. "She didn't used to fight, but she just sits there now too."

"Build your tower, West."

Tests.
Running.
Weight lifting.
Observation.
Always.

"You see that there?"
I could faintly hear them through the glass wall and over the noise the machine around me made.
"Wow," someone else said. "Is that...?"
"Yeah," the other person breathed. "Her bones. They're completely fused with cybernetics."
"That's..." a voice said. "Incredible."
"And look here. Her heart. It looks like it's about seventy-five percent cybernetic as well."
"It would take a lot to stop a heart like that. These girls, they might damn near live forever."
"No one lives forever."
"Are you not seeing what is on this scan?"
"God would not permit anyone to live forever."
"It looks like man has caught up to God if you ask me."

"...kidding me," a voice said through the haze.
"It picked the lock on the southeast entrance."
"That's the second breach in the last week." Margaret. "We'll have to increase the guard."
"We've already got a guard at each entrance at all hours," the man said. "We only have so many bodies."

"Please," I moaned. My vision blurred and swirled. "Stop."

"She's waking up," Margaret said, her voice rising in alarm. "Increase the dosage."

"We're almost out," someone said.

"Then we'd better hurry up."

I walked down the hall, headed back for my room. I'd just finished four hours on the treadmill and Dr. Evans and the people who always watched what we did seemed pleased.

Voices floated through a window as I paused.

West was there, reading a book aloud.

I sat next to him, my face totally blank but looking at the pages.

West turned to me and asked me a question. My eyes met his and I muttered a response and looked back at the book.

West draped his arm around my shoulders and kept reading.

Something bubbled up inside of me, hot and toxic. West was kind and caring with that me. But the real me he pestered and annoyed and tortured and pushed until I exploded.

My fingers curled into fists and tiny black lines flickered across my vision.

I turned and continued down the hall.

"Is it true?" the woman asked.

I'd been in her care for years, but she had never given me her name.

Not that I had ever asked for it.

Dr. Evans nodded, a smile pulling at the corner of his lips as he looked at me. It was the first real looking one I'd seen on his face in years.

"They ran out of funding," he said, turning back to the woman. "They're going to pay for us to keep the Eve project maintained, but we don't have to do any more testing."

"What will you do with them?" she asked, glancing over at me. "They'll never be normal again. Not after this long."

"We'll keep them here," he said, his tone falling once again into seriousness. "This is their home anyway, it's all they've ever known. I've already talked to Dr. Beeson. He's going to maintain them. I assume you are on board to continue in two's care?"

"Of course," she said, looking back at me.

I sat on a chair, my hands resting on my thighs, just observing them. Every time Dr. Beeson did an adjustments, I could sit like this, quiet and still, for hours.

"And what will you do?" she asked, looking at Dr. Evans.

He looked from the woman, back to me. "TorBane needs to be completed. The world deserves to have it finished. I need to make it a priority."

"You're a good man, Dr. Evans," the woman said, touching his arm gently. "You've been placed in some impossible situations, but you're still a good man."

His head sagged just a bit and he blinked at the floor a few times. "I don't know about that anymore."

Dr. Beeson was at his computer again, reading numbers that flashed across his screens. One of his team members looked over his shoulder and they conversed quietly.

I sat in front of me, locked with my eyes. Grey-blue and empty. I blinked at the same time I did.

I scratched my chin, my fingernails causing small skin cells to float down to the ground. I reached up and scratched my chin too, but my skin didn't itch.

"Do you think West will still be allowed to visit?" I asked me.

"I hope not," I said, that thing that was red and prickly rising up inside of me again.

"Why don't you tolerate him?" I asked.

"The woman said some people just naturally don't get along," I responded. "She said that's just how me and him are."

"I like him," I said, blinking.

"Good for you."

Faces I knew taking me outside the building I had never been outside of.

Sunlight that was too bright and too foreign.

A device I was led into and that moved.

Tape over my mouth and around my wrists and ankles.

Darkness.

And then NovaTor's front doors.

My skin hummed.
People screamed.
Bodies were still.
Myself attacking everyone in sight.
Blood all over the floor.
West on the floor.
Dr. Evans Jr. with his hands around my neck.
Dr. Evans saying he would dispose of me.
Lies and secrets.
Dr. Beeson.
And then nothing.

FIFTEEN

It was so cold and so dark.

I could almost feel the mist forming in the air as I exhaled. Moisture covered my skin, dew collecting on me like I was a leaf in the mountains of Eden.

My head lolled to the right, my eyes searching the dark.

There was a faint glow around the door, barely revealing an empty room.

I rolled to my side, the world instantly spinning as I did so. I started heaving, but there was nothing in my stomach to expel.

Bracing a hand on the table, I pushed myself into a lopsided sitting position.

Adrenaline flooded my system when the door slowly creaked open, a sliver of light fell on the floor and wall. But my body was too weak to do anything with it.

"Eve?" someone whispered in the dark.

"Stay away from me." I tried to sound threatening, but my voice was just a hoarse croak.

"It's Tristan," the figure said, stepping inside and closing the door behind him. He set something on the table

135

and then a lantern started to glow softly. He placed a bag next to it and met my eyes. His features were pronounced in the dim light.

"How do you feel?" he asked.

"I could use some water," I managed to get out.

"Of course," he said, reaching into the bag and producing a plastic bottle. He unscrewed the lid and handed it to me. I drank half of it before taking a breath.

"Gunner was supposed to have night watch over you tonight," Tristan said as he pulled some sort of survival food bar from the bag as well. He unwrapped it and handed it to me. I started in on it greedily. "I convinced him to let me switch."

"You don't normally stand guard over me though, do you?" I questioned.

"No," he said, meeting my eyes. "He seemed pretty suspicious, but he was also dozing off."

"Night time then?" I asked, feeling my strength start to return. I flexed my arms and legs and pulled myself into an upright sitting position.

"Yeah," he said, pulling something out of the bag. "About three in the morning."

"How long has it been?" I asked. I realized then it was clothing he'd pulled out of the bag and I was wearing a grimy hospital gown. "How long have I been under?"

"Fourteen days," he said, his voice grave.

"What?!" I shouted without thinking. Tristan instantly hissed for me to keep it down, a finger pressed to his lips.

"I've been out for two weeks?" I said. My head spun again at my spike in hostility.

Tristan nodded, looking back toward the door. It remained closed and the hall quiet.

"What about West?" I asked, my stomach turning cold and hard.

"They did the surgery," Tristan said, turning his attention back to me. "It was pretty rough from what I hear. We only had so much anesthesia since you were under for so long, so they couldn't give him a strong dosage. It wasn't easy for him."

"But they got it out?" I asked. It felt like a snake had wrapped around my heart and lungs, tightening until I heard what I needed confirmed. "The scrap?"

He slowly nodded. "Yeah, they got it."

A relieved sigh escaped my chest and my entire body sagged with it.

"He's in recovery, but it's going to take a while. Like I said, it was pretty rough. He's been drinking a lot of alcohol just to try and dull the pain."

As sorry as I might feel for West that he was in pain, I knew he would survive it. If he could survive TorBane, he could survive the pain.

"Thank you," I said, placing a hand on Tristan's arm.

He nodded again.

"Come on," he said. "We've got to get you dressed before I get you out of here."

"You're going to help me escape?" I questioned, my eyes narrowing at him.

"They've helped your friend," he said, pulling a pair of boots from his bag. "They can't hang that over your head anymore. And...well, they've sewn you up so they must be finished with you."

Suddenly I had to confront what I had been ignoring until that point.

My head was freezing cold.

I raised a tentative hand, my fingers hovering for a long moment. The back of my eyes stung and there was a large lump in my throat.

"Gentle," Tristan said, his expression regretful.

My fingers very first met sticky stitches. And bare skin.

I slowly ran a hand over my head.

They'd shaven every last trace of my hair away.

"What did they do to me?" I whispered, my eyes blurring.

Tristan cleared his throat and his voice was rough when he spoke. "I didn't see any of it," his eyes dropped from mine. "But the stitches run all the way around your head. It looks like they did some serious digging."

And then everything I'd seen while I was under hit me like an anvil to the chest.

Dr. Evans. Both of them. West as a kid. A kid that I hated.

Seeing myself. Talking to myself. Hating myself.

What did that even mean? How far had they broken me that I would be seeing and talking to myself?

"You okay?" Tristan whispered.

"No," I answered, shaking my head as my eyes stared at nothing distinguishable on the floor. "I am not okay."

"Understandable," he said. "But we'd better get moving or we're not going to get you out of here in time."

I nodded, taking a second to try to collect myself.

I stood, only to collapse to the floor.

Tristan swore and helped to pull me to my feet. "I swear I'm not just trying to catch a peek, but it looks like I'm going to have to help you get dressed."

Holding Avian firmly in my mind the entire time, I let Tristan help me stand while I awkwardly pulled the hospital gown off and slid into clothes that weren't mine. I was immensely grateful when I realized the necklace Avian had made me was still around my neck.

"Drink some of this," Tristan said when I was clothed. He handed me another plastic bottle of red liquid. "It tastes like crap, but it will help bring your strength back quicker."

He was right, it was awful. Like liquid sugar. But it instantly flooded my system with energy.

"Come on," he said, slipping one of my arms around his neck and half hauling me out the door.

He dimmed the lamp when we got into the hallway. He turned left down a passageway and we walked silently for about fifty yards. We took a sharp left, and then another immediate right. Tristan opened a door with a set of keys and then locked it again behind us.

The space we were in was large and dark. An old bed was pushed into one corner and a guitar leaned against the wall.

"This is my room," Tristan said, leading me to the bed and easing me onto it. "It's right under an old coffee shop. I opened up the floor to it a few weeks after I joined the Underground. Like you said, there's something not moral about a few people here and I wanted a way out if I needed it, whenever I wanted. No one else knows about it."

I nodded. "Just give me a second."

I placed my hands over my eyes. My fingers were shaking violently.

I was always the one who saved people. I wasn't the one that needed saving. This wasn't who I was.

I took five deep breaths, then sat halfway up.

"You could come with me," I said, meeting his eyes. "You'd fit in in New Eden. The people there aren't perfect, but they're good people."

"You have no idea how tempting that offer is," Tristan said, shaking his head as he looked up at the ceiling. "But there is something else you need to know."

The air grew colder somehow with his heavy words and I knew whatever he said next would be bad.

"I overheard Margaret talking to some of her crew," he started explaining. "That beacon they tried setting off down where you live? They left another one there and they're planning to set it off remotely."

"What?" I growled. "When?"

"New Year's day," he said, his expression darkening. "Margaret is pretty pissed off. Her entire mission seems to have failed, first with getting your colony to cooperate, and second with you. Sounds like they didn't get what they wanted from you."

"New Year's," I breathed. "How far away is that?"

"Thirteen days," Tristan replied.

"What about West?" I asked. "I've got to get him away from these people. West hasn't exactly been pleasant to be around lately, but he shouldn't be here."

Tristan shook his head, pacing the room. "He won't be ready to leave for at least a few more days. You can't wait that long. You've got to warn your people."

"How am I supposed to just leave him here though?" I said, my chest tightening. I was pissed with West for what he'd done, but I wouldn't let them keep swaying him into being a bad human being.

"I'll stay, keep an eye on him. I can't guarantee what Margaret will do when she discovers you're gone. I'll protect him until he's strong enough to travel. Then I'll tell him what happened, the truth. We'll follow you as soon as he's ready."

"And you're sure you'll be able to get the both of you out?" I questioned. Tristan really was a good man if he was willing to protect West, not even knowing him.

"I'm going to try my best." He walked to the far corner of his room and pulled an armoire away from the wall. I saw the dim cut out square in the ceiling.

"I'm sorry, I know you're not at your peak, but we've got to get moving," he said, crossing the space back to his bed. He reached underneath it and pulled out a shotgun and a box of ammunition. "There's only twenty shells left," he explained as he emptied the box into one of my cargo pockets. He also slipped a knife in. "Hopefully it's enough to keep you alive until you can get home."

"I'll make it enough," I said, accepting the shotgun. It was old, but it was going to have to do.

"Come on."

With his help, I climbed on top of the armoire and lifted the board to the floor above.

Dust clouded my lungs from the rug that covered the hidden door. I coughed as quietly as I could manage. Tristan lifted me into the space above.

It seemed to be one of the few buildings in Seattle the Bane didn't occupy. How Tristan had managed that, I didn't know and I wasn't going to risk speaking and calling them to us. Tristan popped up after me, and taking one of my hands in his, led us out of the building.

It was raining lightly and I felt my clothes slowly dampening. Once again, we walked in the middle of the road, up the street, rising away from the water.

We moved slowly and I was getting tired of feeling weak and human. But I kept pace as best I could.

Thankfully, we didn't go far before slowing at the side of a road.

"These are the keys," Tristan said, placing something cold and hard in my hand. He stopped beside a very aggressive looking motorcycle. "This is a bullet bike. It's built for speed but it isn't necessarily built for stability. The roads aren't exactly in good shape these days so you're going to have to be careful. You know how to drive one of these?"

I nodded. Avian had been teaching me how to ride his.

"Good," Tristan said. He kept checking around us but there wasn't much to see. With the overhead clouds, it was incredibly dark. "You're going to head up this block and get on the freeway. This road will lead you right to it. You're going to drive on it for a few hours and watch for the exit for highway 101." He was speaking quickly now as if sensing our window of time was closing. "It will take you straight back to your home and it's a smaller road than the freeway. Smaller cities, less Bane. It'll take you longer than the freeway, but you stand a higher chance of surviving."

"Got it," I said. I stretched my neck from the left to the right. I was starting to feel like my normal self once again. My skin felt tight around my scalp. The stitches were already healing. I'd have to cut them out in a few hours.

"Now, it's probably going to wake the Bane when you start this. It isn't exactly quiet. This might sound a little non-chivalrous, but wait until I get back inside before you start the engine, okay?"

This managed to crack a smile on my lips.

"Chivalry is wasted on someone like me," I said.

This brought a upwards curl to his lips. For the first time, I noticed his bottom teeth were crooked. But unlike Margaret's, which were disgusting, Tristan's were...endearing.

He met my eyes again. "I regret that I haven't gotten the opportunity to get to know you more, Eve," he said. "I can only keep my fingers crossed that I will get the opportunity later."

"Me too," I said, my expression growing serious again. "Thank you. For everything."

"Somehow I have a feeling you're more important than just learning how the Bane came to be. Something tells me you might be able to save us all someday."

"I think you might be overestimating me," I said, shifting uncomfortably from one foot to the other. I wasn't unsure how to deal with his over spoken, very serious statement. "But I appreciate the heroics."

He nodded and clapped a hand on my shoulder.

"Godspeed."

"Stay safe," I said back.

Tristan then turned, and jogged back toward the coffee shop.

I'd counted my steps on our way here and translated them to seconds.

That's exactly how long I waited before roaring the motorcycle to life.

A brilliant beam of light shot through the dark, directly into a window. The Bane inside instantly crashed through the glass.

I gunned the gas, and shot straight toward them.

I wasn't left handed, and since I only had one hand to shoot with, I missed the first shot. The three Bane rushing me grew closer as I rocketed toward them.

I fired again, taking one of them down.

The other two were closing in on me when I turned sharply to the left, down an alley. It was barely wide enough for the bike to fit through, but keeping my balance and the handlebars straight, I leaned flat against the bike and rocketed between buildings.

I took the next right I could and got back onto the main road, the one Tristan had said would lead to the freeway.

I glanced over my shoulder and saw a dozen Bane already sprinting down the street after me. The light drizzle above wasn't enough to keep them indoors.

But they weren't as fast as the bike beneath me and they soon fell behind. The headlight illuminated a green sign with directions to the onramp for I-5. I had to slow momentarily as I climbed the ramp. The road was badly cracked and dropping away in sections.

The freeway practically sang to me as I reached it and pushed the bike past ninety miles an hour.

"I'm coming, Avian," I breathed.

SIXTEEN

All along the freeway there was city after city. I saw Bane waking to life off the side of the road, but by the time they reached it, I was long gone. The Bane were fast, but this bike's speedometer read over one hundred miles an hour when I really pushed it.

I realized just how far I'd been taken north by how much longer it took the sun to faze into the sky. It was also nearly the end of December and the days were at their shortest. I had turned off the freeway onto Tristan's highway 101 for a half hour before the sun started lightening the world. The air was crisp and had I been normal, I would be freezing with the thin jacket Tristan had brought me. The moisture in the air hung between the point of dew and frost.

A tiny costal town had just fallen behind me when I decided it was time to hide for the day. I left the motorcycle on the side of the road, next to an abandoned bus, and headed into the trees. The scarce grass crunched under my feet as the temperatures hovered at freezing.

Finding an ancient maple tree, I climbed high into its branches and settled.

Taking out the pocket knife Tristan had given me, I felt along the crown of my head. The stitches were pulling tight. The incision line was completely healed. I tried not to wonder if they had pulled my entire scalp off to dig in my brain. Or if they cut the top of my skull off…

Trying my best to be careful, I slipped the small knife under the thread, and cut.

Small trickles of blood traced their way down my face and neck by the time I was done, but I cut each of the stitches and piled them on the branch.

The back of my throat swelled.

I'd never given much thought to my hair before. Many times it had felt like a nuisance, always getting in my vision.

But for the first time in my life, I actually felt ugly.

My hair was now shorter than Avian's. And Avian very nearly didn't have hair with how frequently he shaved it.

How long would it take to grow back?

I collected myself after a few minutes. I had to survive a fifteen-hundred-mile journey. I didn't have time to mourn the loss of something as silly and unnecessary as hair.

The sun broke over the tops of the trees, and through them, I could just barely make out the ocean.

It seemed Tristan was right. This highway literally ran right next to the ocean, and so far, there had only been small towns along it. Towns small enough to not even have any Bane in them.

But I was grossly underprepared for this journey. I had no idea what had happened to my pack. In a way that almost felt like losing an arm. I would have been just fine if I'd had that. Now I had no food, no water. I had no extra clothing and I was nearly soaked through. I had none of my familiar firearms and this shotgun Tristan had given me wasn't exactly in prime condition.

I was going to have to raid one of these towns. And search for gas before too long.

As badly as I wanted to deny it, my body was exhausted. The raid would have to wait. I didn't last much more than a few minutes before I drifted off.

⊱━━━━⊰

A bird squawked. I opened one eye and saw it standing on the branch above me. It looked right at me, so focused and so precise it didn't even really look like a real bird. I didn't recognize its species; he must have been native to this area. But he was big.

My stomach rumbled. I had no idea if the people in Seattle had starved me those fourteen days they'd had me under or not, but I was famished.

And that bird looked like a meal.

Moving very slowly, I pulled the knife from my pocket. I opened the blade and pinched it very carefully between my index finger and thumb.

I flicked the blade and threw it before the bird could even blink. The knife embedded itself in the creature's throat and he dropped from the branch.

A smile threatening to cross my face, I pulled myself half into a sitting position, about to jump off the branch and retrieve my meal when I froze.

At least twenty Bane stood at the base of the tree. Just staring up at me.

A curse slipped over my lips as I scrambled higher up the tree. Branches and bark scraped my skin, but I felt nothing as I fled, trapping myself in the tree. I leveled my shotgun at the nearest Bane.

But they didn't move. They didn't blink.

They just stood there staring at me.

My heart thundered in my chest. My breaths came in quick spurts. My hands grew slick with sweat.

Why weren't they attacking?

Why weren't they acting like Bane?

What were they waiting for?

And then one of them raised an arm, straight up towards me. Clutched in its hand was a water bottle.

Another one raised its arm as well. It held a can of baked beans.

Another held up a handgun and another a box of ammunition.

And another gripped a backpack.

One held up a gas can that sloshed.

"What is going on?" I whispered. My eyes grew wide, my grip on the branches I clung to tightening. "How…?"

They continued to stand there, looking up at me with their empty eyes.

I'd thought about every one of these things before I'd fallen asleep. I knew I was going to have to go after these supplies if I was going to survive.

And these Bane had brought every single thing I'd needed.

"Put them on the ground," I said, my voice cracking on the word ground.

Every one of them put their items in the dirt at their feet.

"Back up," I said, climbing down one branch tentatively.

The entire group stepped back *exactly* ten steps.

"What…?" I whispered. I'd been able to control one or two Bane at a time before. But there were twenty-four of them here, and they'd obeyed me precisely.

And somehow they'd known exactly what I'd needed.

I climbed down a few more branches, watching them the entire time I moved. I kept my shotgun aimed at them, but they just stood there, watching me as I descended.

I dropped to the hard ground, just in front of their stash.

They just continued to stare at me.

Had I finally become enough like them that they no longer felt the need to try and infect me? Were they recognizing me as one of their own?

But they wouldn't bring supplies to one of their own. The Bane would have no use for them.

"Lift your arms," I said hesitantly, keeping my shotgun pointed at them.

Every one of them instantly raised their arms to the sky.

"Holy…" I breathed, shaking my head. I took another step closer, stepping over the backpack. "Turn around once."

They all turned in a full circle before facing me again.

"Now leave," I said, keeping the shotgun pointed at them. "Head north, and don't come back."

Instantly they turned as one and marched north. I watched as they retreated through the woods. None of them looked back.

I stood there, stunned, long after they disappeared from sight.

This was new. This was game-changing in a way that I didn't really understand yet. This could either hurt us or maybe save us.

Either way, the world of the post-Evolution was changing once again.

Turning back to the scattered supplies, I grabbed a can opener one of the Bane had brought and opened the beans. They felt cold and slimy as they went down, but they calmed the rumbling in my stomach.

More than one of them had brought water. I counted six water bottles. I drained one and packed the rest into the backpack. I tried to ignore the math homework and diary I had to pull out of it and discard.

I grabbed the handgun and checked the ammunition. They'd brought the right kind. The Bane really were getting smarter. They'd checked to make sure it was the right caliber.

There was other food as well. Granola bars, all of which were moldy and rotten when I opened the wrappers. Guess the Bane weren't smart enough to make sure the food was edible. But there were two cans of green beans that were still good, as well as three cans of soup. I loaded it all into the backpack.

Peeling off my soaked clothes, I changed into the dry ones. They were too big—men's—but they were military grade and durable.

I left the dead bird, now sorry for needlessly killing it, and collected Tristan's knife.

I walked back out to the road and my motorcycle, gas can in hand. I looked both ways. The road was empty.

Judging from the position of the sun in the sky, I would guess it was four in the afternoon. I'd slept for a long time. I shuttered to think how long the Bane might have waited below me, watching me while I slept with supplies I needed, but hadn't told them to collect.

I couldn't sleep any longer and there was no way I was going to sit around and wait until dark. Strapping the pack to my back tight, I topped off the motorcycle with the gas. It didn't require much and I had plenty left over once it was full. Finding some ties in the tiny storage compartment in the back of the bike, I strapped the gas can on for when I would need it later.

The motorcycle growled to life and I took off down the coast.

This had to be an advantage for me, for New Eden. The way the Bane had listened to me was precise. There was no hesitation in their obedience. They'd gotten exactly what I'd needed without me saying a word.

There had to be a way I could use this to help me get home. To protect those around me.

It started raining not five minutes after I got back on the road. I was soaked once again in under a minute. It was a relief to not have my hair sticking to my face from the rain, but my head was freezing cold.

The rain would start and stop for the next hour but the gray clouds overhead never left.

Something loomed ahead and I wiped the water from my eyes, trying to see what was coming up.

It looked like there was a big river or maybe a bay ahead of me. A bridge stretched over a huge expanse of water and on the other side there looked to be a town. I started across.

Just then, the sun broke from the clouds and the rain stopped.

And as soon as the sun broke, Bane erupted from every building, every car, and every overhang.

I screeched to a halt on the bridge, the back tire of the bike lifting slightly. My chest bumped the fuel tank as I slid forward with my abrupt stop.

The ground looked like it was moving, constantly shifting, there were so many bodies. There had to be hundreds of thousands of Bane. I'd seen a sign as I hit the halfway point on the bridge, a sign that had said some town name and listed the population as just under ten-thousand.

These Bane had come from somewhere else.

I narrowed my enhanced eyes, trying to make sense of what I was seeing.

Batches of them crushed cars to flat metal disks. Others broke windows, and things started flying out them as they ransacked the buildings. And then the explosions started.

Building after building started coming down.

They moved like clockwork. Thousands of them moved in a direct line, going block by block, searching each building and then leveling it.

A small flash of light caught my eyes. There were five Bane standing in a line behind the others, in a straight line. But these looked different from the others. They literally had no flesh left on their frames. Metallic bones held in pulsing and ticking organs.

"What are you doing out there? Are you trying to get infected?"

My head whipped to the right, toward a hissing voice.

A pair of brown eyes peaked up at me from the side of the bridge, down on the small beach at the land and water's edge. He waved me over.

Glancing back at the unbelievable scene before me, I climbed off my bike, leaving it in the middle of the road, and ran to the man's hiding place.

"What are you doing out here?" I asked as I ducked under the road next to him.

He was dressed in survival gear and had one rifle and one shotgun crossed over his back. He held a crossbow in one hand.

"Studying," he said, his voice gruff. He looked to be in his forties, wrinkles sprouting from the corners of his eyes. His hair was shaggy, his beard knotted and tangled.

"What's that supposed to mean?" I asked.

"Something's changing out there," he said, his expression growing dark. "I first noticed it in Minneapolis. You saw those freaky looking ones? The ones with no traces of skin on them?"

I nodded.

"They're first gens," he said, his eyes glancing back toward the road, and then back to me. "The source. They were the first ones to get TorBane."

"How do you know?" I questioned.

154

"Because one of them is my father," he said, his jaw tightening. "He got a heart upgrade in the beginning. I'd been overseas in the Navy when all this happened. When I got back, he'd already lost his humanity. A lot of people had. So I watched him. I've been tracking him for the past six years. He's one of the first gens."

"Okay," I said, nodding. It made sense. The longer you were infected, the more machine-like you became. I'd already seen that.

"Two other first gens found him about three months ago," the man said, again looking toward the road. "They started going through houses and tearing them apart. And I mean *leveling* them. They've been looking for people, anyone who's left. And as they moved through the city, any awake Bane they came across went with them. They started growing an army. All the others, they seem to be following the first gens."

"Hang on," I said, holding a hand up. "That can't be possible. The Bane cannot be smart enough to create an army."

"Did you not just see what is happening in that town?" he asked, his eyes blazing. He pointed a finger toward the city. "Can you not call that an army?"

I swore under my breath. He was right. It was an army.

"They're moving like the black plague," he continued. "They're marching in a line, perfectly east to west. They're leveling houses, forests, anything that might hide people. And anyone they find, they infect. They're thinking like a machine. They're doing precise sweeps."

"They've reached the coast now," I said, trying to bring up a map I'd seen of or continent. "What do you think they'll do now?"

"I expect they'll turn, make a sweep west to east until they reach the east coast. If they're really thinking like a machine, that's how a machine would do it."

"And you've what?" I asked. "You've just been following them?"

He nodded. "I have an all-terrain vehicle," he said, inclining his head back toward the city. "I've been trying to get out ahead of them, find anyone I can. Warn them to get out."

"Have you found anyone?" I asked, hope surging in my chest.

His eyes grew dark. "I've come across five people, in two different locations. I told them to head north. My guess is that they'll shift south now that they've reached the coast."

"How long do you think it'll take them to reach Los Angeles?" I asked, fear gripping my chest.

He took a deep breath before letting it out slowly as he shook his head. "No for sure way to tell. I'm guessing they'll continue sweeping east to west, west to east. They're gaining speed. They keep collecting more Bane as they move, and they haven't even hit any major cities yet. I can't imagine how their numbers are going to grow when they hit Chicago or Portland. Or, shit, New York. The more Bane they have, the faster they can work and the wider the sweep they can do."

"How long?" I asked again.

"I'd guess six months," he said with a shrug. "But probably shorter. They could have hundreds of millions of them by the time they hit Los Angeles. Why do you ask about that location?"

I hesitated. My trust in mankind was greatly compromised after what had just happened to me in Seattle. However, this man hadn't asked me any questions before spilling all of his information.

"Because that's where I'm from. There are over one hundred of us living there. There are probably still more in hiding."

"Wow," he said, his eyes growing wider. "That's the biggest colony I've heard of."

"And it's going to be obliterated if that many Bane show up to level it," I said quietly, my thoughts racing.

We had to get the Pulse ready for more than one reason now.

We needed to build more of it if possible.

"If you're from Los Angeles, what are you doing this far north?" he asked. Suddenly his eyes jumped to my hair line. "And what happened to you, child?"

"Some of us humans are getting desperate," I said with my jaw clenched.

"It was one of *us* that did that?" he asked, disgust in his voice.

I nodded.

"I'm sorry to hear it," he said, his eyes growing softer. "What's your name?"

"Eve," I said.

"I'm Tom," he offered, shifting the firearms on his back.

"Nice to meet you, Tom," I said. And I meant it. In a way, Tom reminded me of Bill. A little rough around the edges, but at his core, he was a good man.

He simply gave a smile and a nod in return.

We hid there the rest of the day, sharing what information we each had. But neither of us learned anything new. The Bane were Evolving, they'd soon take us over.

The sound of destruction from the town never stopped.

There were explosions almost constantly. Tom said they managed to find explosives wherever they went, but much of the sounds we were hearing were gas lines being broken and lit. There were grinding sounds as buildings came down and homes and businesses were destroyed.

"Did you find anyone here?" I asked. The Bane had moved to the south end of the city and he and I sat on the bank, watching the destruction. Half the city burned, sending plumes of smoke into the sky.

Tom shook his head.

"When those people took me," I said, running a hand over my bald head. "They told me there was less than half a percent left of the human population left."

"That sounds about right," Tom said, shaking his head.

"Something's got to happen soon or we're done for."

"I've kept thinking that someday someone would come and light the way, to have the answers and this would all end," Tom said, his voice growing quiet. "Seems it's too late for that now."

I remembered Tristan's words. About me being the key to saving them all.

No matter how much I wished I could save this planet, I didn't see how that could ever be possible.

Evening started to fall and the sounds grew less intense.

"That's my cue to leave," Tom said, standing. "I don't normally linger this long. I'd better get moving. There's always another town."

I stood as well, tightening the pack on my back. "Thank you, Tom. You might have just saved my family."

"I'll keep warning people until I get caught," he said, giving a shrug. "I'll use this on myself though before I let myself turn." He patted his shotgun.

"Stay safe, Tom," I said with a nod.

He saluted me and started down the road. He didn't go far before he climbed onto an ATV I hadn't even noticed. It was well camouflaged with neutral paint. The engine growled and he took off.

I watched for an hour on the beach. Then there was no city left. Only rubble and smoke.

The army of Bane started marching east, just as Tom had predicted.

SEVENTEEN

It was dark before I dared head out. I turned the headlight on the motorcycle and started walking it through the cluttered street. It took me a long time to make my way through. Broken glass threatened to pop the tires. Busted concrete that was once part of some building blocked the way.

But finally I made it to the other side, back into open trees and clear road.

There were trees. Endless trees. More trees than I could even imagine.

There were tiny towns.

And there was the endless ocean to my right that gave me hope that I would be seeing my family soon. This was the same ocean Avian and I lived next to. Somehow that made him seem not so far away.

Hours passed and one state became another.

And I started seeing signs that made me pause.

Redwoods National Forest.

Where the Seattle people claimed they were from.

Lies.

The trees here were ancient, towering. They blocked out the starlight, creating a dark tunnel. The temperature dropped and the world grew eerily quiet. A barely-there skiff of snow covered the branches and ground.

My speed must have been pushing eighty miles per hour, so when the hulking object in the middle of the overgrown road came into my limited view, I didn't have enough time to stop.

I slammed on the breaks and swerved just a little too hard to the right. Losing traction on the frosty road, the back tire came up as the bike turned and I was on the ground, sliding with the bike. We both slammed into something metal and large.

Gingerly picking myself off the ground, I saw what looked a lot like a track wheel where the motorcycle illuminated the object in the dark. I righted the mangled motorcycle, backing up to give light to the entire mass.

The words NEW EDEN were painted in big, bold, black letters on the side of the tank.

"Avian!" I screamed. "Royce? Gabriel!"

Adrenaline burned through my system and for the first time in the last three weeks, I felt truly alive again.

I dragged the motorcycle back, making the circle of light larger. I jumped up on the track wheel and climbed up to the hatch.

"Avian!" I yelled again as I struggled with the lock. "Bill?"

Finally unlocking it, I heaved the hatch open and peered into the dark.

"Hello?"

But only silence answered me.

I dropped down inside, my eyes struggling to adjust to the nearly nonexistent light. "Hello?"

My blood grew cold.

Grappling through the dark, my fingers found a flashlight and I flipped it on.

The interior of the tank was devoid of life.

Where were they?

I pulled my upper half back up through the hatch of the tank, staring out into the silent night.

"Hello?" I bellowed. "Is anyone out there?"

The trees were silent.

I dropped back into the tank. The light from the flashlight reflected off of something on the floor and I bent to inspect it. It was dark drops of blood and for a moment I was about to go into full panic mode for my family's safety, when more drops fell to the floor and I realized it was my own. I shined the light on my right arm and found it ground to pieces. Small bits of gravel were embedded in my skin.

Ignoring it for the moment, I swept the flashlight through the interior of the tank again.

It was difficult to tell how many members of New Eden had come in the tank. It was an empty shell that offered no clues.

They could have gotten raided by marauders. But I doubted that. There weren't many people left in general and anyone who would have come after me would now how to handle themselves.

They could have been found by the Bane, but I doubted that too. There would be nothing about this area that would attract the Bane. Not that there wasn't a chance they tracked into the area, but I didn't think that was it.

It circled back to the reason the tank had to be here. The Seattle people had said they were from the Redwoods. New Eden had come after me. Whatever supplies they'd brought with them they took out with them to go look for me.

They were out there. Somewhere.

And I had no doubt that Avian was with them.

I sat on the lip of the hatch the rest of that night, my shotgun ready in my lap. I listened for any trace of sound, but the trees and moss that surrounded me killed any noise.

The sun started creeping through the morning haze, washing the earth in gray light.

While I'd waited for morning to come, I strategized. There had to be thousands of square miles in these forests. Avian and the others could be anywhere.

But there was only one place they'd left the tank.

And eventually they had to come back to it.

I made a small fire as soon as it was light enough for me to find wood that might burn. It was nearly impossible to get it started. Everything here was wet from the snow and I didn't have a proper flint. But after a half hour of trying, I finally got a small flame.

I blackened one end of a stick and when it was charcoaled enough, I took that end to the side of the tank.

I'm here. Be back at sun down. Wait. -Eve

I stepped back when I was finished writing, making sure it was noticeable enough.

They couldn't miss it if they came back to the tank.

Dropping the stick off the side of the road and smothering the fire I'd worked so hard to start, I set out through the trees.

I headed east off the highway. If there really was a hiding colony like the Seattle people were supposed to have, that would be the logical direction for a camp. But they wouldn't go more than a few days from the road and ocean. They would stick to their resources, just like we had back in the mountains.

It made my heart ache as I hiked through the forest. I had missed nature. I had missed trees and moss and soft earth. If I had a choice, I would choose to live in a place like this. Not in a city with endless buildings and concrete.

"Avian!" I shouted every so often as I hiked. "Royce? Bill? Tuck?"

But no one responded.

As the sky started to darken, I made my way back to the tank. My heart started beating faster as I moved back in its direction. I imagined how I would react if I found Avian there, waiting for me. The back of my eyes stung and my chest constricted.

But he wasn't there when I reached the tank. No one was.

How long had the tank been sitting there? They could have come looking for me as soon as they realized I was gone. I didn't know how long the fighting had gone on after they'd taken me, but I couldn't imagine it was long. There had been a fairly large crew when we returned to Seattle. It probably took Avian three or four days to get from New Eden to the forest.

They could have been trooping through these trees for two weeks now.

It might be a few more weeks before they came back to the tank. And I didn't have that kind of time to wait.

I slept on the hard road that night, again ever grateful that I didn't feel pain. I tried not shiver the entire time.

In the morning I hiked through the woods. The sun came out and melted the snow.

Again I found no one.

I slept on the road again. Fear started creeping up in my stomach. What if they couldn't get back to the tank? What if they'd been injured? What if the Bane really were out in these woods? We'd been driven out of our own mountains because they'd pressed so far into the wilderness before.

When morning came, a thought occurred to me. I'd called Bane I hadn't meant to call before. Why couldn't I do it again? If there was a chance there were Bane in this forest, I could do the one thing I could to protect whoever from New Eden might be out there.

I focused all my thoughts, channeled my energy or whatever I thought would help, into calling the Bane to me.

Today I would wait at the tank.

I stood just in front of it, my shotgun ready. And I waited.

The first one came an hour after I started the call. It came out of the woods twenty yards south of the tank onto the road. It headed directly up the road toward me, its dead eyes fixed on me.

It took only two shells to kill it. It dropped in the middle of the road.

Another came out of the woods, right in front of me, three hours later. He was so close before I saw him emerge from the woods that it only took one shot to take him down.

As the time continued to pass, my stomach started to growl, reminding me that I hadn't eaten anything in more than twenty-four hours.

I'd just taken off my pack and was digging through it for one of the cans of soup when I heard shots being fired.

"Avian!" I bellowed, instantly sprinting through the trees toward the sounds.

"Eve?" I heard him yell, probably two hundred yards away.

Seven more shots were fired, shouts rose into the air, and then they ceased.

"Avian!" I screamed again. I was rocketing through the trees at this point.

And suddenly he came into view. Fifty yards away through the trees. He was running in my direction too.

His step faltered when his eyes found me. Horror filled his face.

But he crushed me into his chest when we finally collided.

"What the hell did they do to you?" he growled into the curve of my neck. I looked up into his eyes to see them burning with hatred. He inspected my hairline and the still fresh scar I knew was there.

166

"I'm okay," I said, shaking my head, then laying my cheek on his chest and squeezing him tighter. Avian's hand hesitantly came to the back of my head as he embraced me.

"Eve?" I heard Gabriel's voice a ways away. I turned from Avian to see who else had come to find me.

Gabriel, Bill, and Tuck came towards us through the woods.

There were two Bane lying dead in a heap, their bodies riddled with bullet holes.

"They didn't try to hurt anyone, did they?" I asked, looking back at Avian.

"No," Avian shook his head. "They were just marching through the trees. That's what caught our attention. They walked right past us and didn't even acknowledge we were there. We followed them but didn't dare let them get any closer to the tank."

"It was me," I said, my voice lowered. Gabriel, Bill, and Tuck stopped at our sides. "They were heading here because of me."

"What do you mean?" Gabriel asked.

"I was waiting for you all to come back to the tank," I said, looking each of them over for damage. They all looked fine. "I've been waiting for two days. But…something's changed. The people who took me? They did something to me."

Avian swore under his breath. "What'd they do?" His eyes were pained.

For some reason I felt ashamed for what had happened. I was too strong to let them do something like this to me. "They were trying to figure out the reason why I can't be infected. I think they thought they could find a cure. I don't know if they found what they were looking for, but they did something else while they were in there. And I don't think they realized they did it."

"What is it, Eve?" Avian asked, his voice low.

"You know how I could control the Bane before?" I asked, looking around to Gabriel, Bill, and Tuck. "Just one or two of them?"

They each nodded.

"It's exponentially stronger now," I said, my eyes growing dark. "I was trying to call any Bane that might be in the forest, to keep them away from you until I could find you."

"But you were so far away," Tuck said, his eyes narrowing at me. "How is that possible?"

"I don't know," I said. I told them about how I had only thought of the supplies I needed to survive, and how the next morning the Bane had collected them for me.

"This changes things," Bill said. "I'm not exactly sure how, but it changes things."

I nodded in agreement.

"One more thing," I said, looking back at Avian. "Those people who invaded New Eden. They're not here. Someone helped me escape, but West is still in Seattle."

"You've been in Seattle all this time?" Avian gaped, anger blazing in his eyes again. He shook his head, his fists balling.

"What about West?" Gabriel asked. "Did he turn? He's supposed to have gone back in for Extraction by now."

"They said they'd help him," I said. "They promised their doctor would get the scrap out of his heart and that he'd be TorBane-free. They told me the surgery worked. The man who helped me get out, he said he would bring West as soon as he was well enough to travel."

"Do you trust them?" Bill asked. "Do you trust them that they won't kill him once they realize you're gone?"

"Them, no," I said shaking my head. "The man who helped me, yes. He said he'd protect West until then."

"This is his fault, isn't it?" Avian growled. His expression darkened. "He told them about you, didn't he?"

I closed my eyes and shook my head, pushing my emotions down. "It doesn't matter now. I'm back. I'm okay."

"Oh, it matters," he hissed.

"Avian," Gabriel chided. "You've got to get over this anger towards him. It's not going to do anyone any good."

"West could have gotten her killed, Gabriel!" Avian shouted. "Look at her!"

"But like she said," Gabriel spoke, his voice rising slightly. "She's back now."

Avian gave a big sigh, his body slumping as the fight went out of him. He wrapped his arms around me again, crushing me into his chest. Suddenly Gabriel wrapped his arms around the two of us and I was sandwiched in the middle.

"I was worried you were gone to us," Gabriel said in his rough voice. "You've made it through too much to be taken out by humans."

"I'm okay," I said again. But I wasn't really sure it was true.

"Any idea what this is?" Bill asked and his finger lightly touched the back of my scalp.

"What?" I asked.

"You've got a roman numeral two tattooed to the back of your head," Bill said. Avian turned me so he could inspect it himself.

"That's not fresh," Avian said. "That's old ink."

"Who knows," I said, shaking my head and turning around again. I took one of Avian's hands and one of Gabriel's. "I just want to go home now."

"Let's head back to the tank," Avian said, looking down at me. He pressed a kiss to my forehead. "We'll head home in the morning."

EIGHTEEN

I sat across from Avian, simply looking at him, still not quite believing that I'd found him, so far from home. Against the odds, we'd found each other again.

But something in me knew that I would always find Avian.

Gabriel, Bill, and Tuck had offered to sleep outside. At first I had blushed. I didn't feel embarrassed often, but the thought of them just outside the steel walls made my face warm.

But as I sat across the tank from Avian, I was grateful for their offer.

"I took off on my own at first," Avian said, his eyes never breaking away from mine. "As soon as I realized they took you, I grabbed an emergency pack and a gun and just took off. Gabriel caught up to me twenty minutes later in the tank."

I shook my head, a real smile pulling at my lips. "That wasn't very smart."

A smile flitted across his own face. "I tend to lose my head when it comes to you."

That happy expression finally spread on my face. "How does stuff like this happen?" I asked. I felt silly for the grin on my face. "How does fate align perfectly that I find Eden, a place safe with good people who could help to mold me into the person I've become? That I find you? That I get taken across the country and the moment I escape, find my way back to you?"

Avian's eyes grew dark and serious but they danced like stars reflecting on water. He stood and crossed the space toward me. He nudged my legs apart with his knee, standing between them. He placed a hand behind my neck. The gesture felt strange now. His hand should have been tangled in my hair.

"Because sometimes there are two people in this world who are bigger than fate. Sometimes there are two people who are just a force of nature and against all odds, a force this strong cannot be denied."

"I missed you, Avian," I whispered as his forehead touched mine.

"I nearly died without you," he said, his lips only a whisper away from mine. I felt all of his anger and his desperation in that moment and understood them. We were all each other had left in this world.

"Never again," I said, making a promise I knew I would do everything in my power to keep.

"I will always find you."

And finally, he kissed me.

It nearly brought a sob from my chest. I hadn't allowed myself to accept it before, but I had feared I would never be in this place again. I had nearly lost us forever.

This was me, the unchangeable, unbreakable part of me.

Avian's lips weren't gentle. They were desperate and they were lonely. They were fearful and possessive. His teeth tugged on my bottom lip. His breathing came out ragged.

My hands slid under his shirt, my fingers feeling alive and electric as they passed over his toned abdomen. I pushed his shirt up and pulled it up over his head. Goosebumps instantly flashed over his skin.

He let me look at him for a moment and I drank him in. His chest was tight and sculpted. Coming to New Eden had done glorious things for his already beautiful body. With more food and free time to do things more challenging than doctoring, he had the body of a god.

My eyes settled on the tattoo of three birds on his chest. My fingers rose to touch the one with the shape of an "S" in the way its wings met its body.

"I love you, Avian," I said. It was a moment before my eyes left the bird and returned to his. "I don't exist as a whole without you."

Avian's eyes burned as he looked back at me through the dim light. He took one of my hands in his and pulled me to my feet. His arms wrapped around my waist and he rested his forehead against mine.

"I promise you my forever," Avian said, pressing a soft and gentle kiss to each of my eyelids.

"My forever is yours to keep," I returned, pulling myself into his chest. I buried my face in his neck, clinging to his frame and breathing him in. I felt his heart beating into my own chest.

There was a fire building between the two of us that night.   A fire that had never burned so bright until that moment, but would continue to burn for that forever we'd promised.   Because that promise of forever, that was my word, my bond, and my eternal will.

NINETEEN

In the morning I told everyone about the other beacon, which was to be set off New Year's day. This sent everyone into action and we immediately rolled south.

I felt like the slow journey would kill me. The motorcycle I'd taken from Seattle was wrecked when I crashed into the tank. We had no choice but to all take the trek home in the tank. It had taken them three days to get here, it was going to take us three days to get home. There was nothing we could do about it. We would get home with seven days to spare. In that time, the scientists would have to rebuild the energy storage devices and get the Pulse charge up. There was zero room for error.

"There is something else you need to know," I said, loud enough so everyone could hear me over the sound of the track wheels. Tuck glanced down at me, he drove the tank. Avian, Bill, and Gabriel turned their full attention to me.

"The Bane, we've known for a few months that they're getting smarter," I started. "But the first generation receivers of TorBane, all the others are following them. They're building an army."

"How is that possible?" Gabriel questioned. "An army of Bane?"

I shook my head. "I don't know exactly, but they're thinking logically. The day before I found the tank, I was about to head through this city when all of the sudden hundreds of thousands of Bane came crawling out and started leveling the city. It was a small town so I knew they had to be coming from somewhere else.

"There was this man," I continued. "He'd been following them, studying them. He said they're sweeping. They're leveling everything, looking for people. They're moving west to east. When they reach the coast they turn south."

"How long till they reach New Eden?" Avian asked, his brow furrowing.

"Tom was estimating maybe six months," I said, the weight of my words filling the interior of the tank. "But he thought it would probably be less. They're gaining numbers as they go. Any Bane that are awake, any Hunters, they're joining the army."

"Well that's as scary as anything I could imagine," Tuck said, shaking his head.

"There aren't nearly as many Sleepers," Gabriel said, rubbing a hand over his once again overgrown beard. "They're all starting to wake up. Millions of them."

"We're going to have to prepare," I said, nodding. "We've got to get the Pulse back up and running. And if possible, I think we need to build others."

"If it's true and they are gaining numbers as they move, there will be over three hundred million of them by the time the reach New Eden," Avian said. "Even if we have multiple Pulses, will it be enough?"

"It will have to be," Bill said. "What other choice would we have?"

"We could move," Tuck suggested.

"Not again," Gabriel shook his head. "There are too many of us now in New Eden. We have a perfect set up there. We will fight back."

"Besides, it isn't like the rest of the country is going to be totally Bane-free," I said, looking up at Tuck. "There *are* still thousands of Sleepers out there. Eventually they're going to wake up, after the army has left."

Tuck sighed, shaking his head. He muttered something about good things never lasting.

"One more thing," I said. I fidgeted with the shotgun that sat in my lap. "I don't think it's safe for me to go back into New Eden. I have no idea what those people did to me, but it seems the Bane might be attracted to me now. I think it's safer for me to hang out on the outskirts. You all can go back in and send Dr. Beeson out to me. He can check me out, see what he thinks."

"Eve..." Avian started to argue.

"You know it can't be safe," I said, shaking my head at him. "We can't risk the Bane following me into the city."

"He'll fix it," Gabriel said. "I've never met a man smarter than Erik."

"Let's hope so," I said with a sigh. But something inside of me wasn't so sure.

We drove through the night and fueled up when the sky was darkest. I took most of the night shift, finally fully recovered from my imprisonment and surgery. Avian slept with his hand on my calf, as if he was afraid I would disappear on him again.

By morning we were reaching cities.

Bill kept track of where we were on his maps. We'd been lucky to have forests to the north. There weren't many cities. But the trees were falling away and the buildings were rising around us.

"I think it's about time for you to head up," Bill said, his finger tracing along the paper. "It all starts here."

Avian met my eyes and where in the past there would have been fear, there was admiration and confidence. He gave me a lopsided smile and pressed a kiss to my forehead. "Go save the world some more," he said.

I couldn't help the full smile that spread on my face. I checked my magazine, loaded my pockets with more ammunition, and opened the hatch.

There were still trees around us but they weren't the towering ancient guardians of the north. These were smaller and more ragged. They had to struggle a little harder for survival.

There was a gas station up ahead and a few shops. There were blocks of houses.

The tank kept rolling through the morning light.

I raised my rifle to eye level, my finger poised on the trigger.

We clattered into the edges of the town. And almost as if it had trumpeted our arrival, bodies stepped into the light.

I started firing as the first batch of twenty sprang at us. Two bodies dropped to the ground with a scraping of metal on concrete.

"Stay back!" I bellowed as the crowd grew and rushed us.

The two hundred plus bodies that were swarming us instantly stopped and took a few steps back.

"You guys want to see this?" I said loud enough those below would be able to hear.

The tank slowed to a stop and I shifted to the side so the others could emerge.

The crowd of Bane just stood before us, twitching and shifting like they wanted to break from my hold the instant I dropped it. But they didn't come any closer.

"Holy..." Bill whispered.

"There are hundreds of them," Gabriel mused. "Why is it so strong now?"

"They did some serious digging in there," I said, keeping my shotgun leveled at the crowd. So did the rest of the team. "I don't think they meant to do this though. I think it is just an unexpected side effect of whatever it was they did to me."

"They're standing back, this many of them," Avian said, holding a hand up to shield the sun from his eyes. "How many of them do you think would listen?"

"We'll find out soon," Bill said. "The next big city after this is San Francisco. Population eight hundred thousand."

"There's no way I can hold off that many of them," I said, shaking my head.

"But hopefully they're not going to all come at us at once," Gabriel said. "We made it through fine in the night when we came up here. We'll make it through again."

How could they be so confident in me? They didn't know what I was capable of anymore. *I* didn't even know what I was capable of.

But those Bane before we were still standing there, just looking at us. Waiting for orders.

"March west," I shouted. "Don't stop when you get to the water."

And as one, the growing crowd turned to their left and started marching, their strides perfectly in unison.

"Not possible," Gabriel whispered as his eyes followed them.

"Welcome to the new age," Avian said. His hand rose to my shoulder and gave a squeeze.

There were Sleepers inside the buildings, just staring out at the world. But not a single Bane moved as we rolled through the town.

It was an exact replay when we reached the next three small towns. But each town got a little bigger. And I sent more and more Bane marching toward the Pacific Ocean.

At noon day, the Golden Gate Bridge was looming before us.

"Maybe we should go around the city," Gabriel said, as we approached. He, Bill, Avian, and I were perched atop the tank while Tuck continued to drive.

Bill shook his head. "That could take us another full day. Probably more. We can't afford to lose any time."

We were all quiet for a moment. I was trying to ignore my self-doubt. Trying to ignore the urgency to get back to New Eden as soon as possible.

"I've got an idea," I suddenly said. "The Bane, they really don't like water. The more Evolved they get, the more so. I saw it while I was in Seattle. It would rain and they were a lot more hesitant to come out. A lot of them would die just stepping out in the rain.

"If I can call as many of them out as I can onto that bridge, I can make them jump off. The water will kill most of them."

"And you're sure they won't rip you apart?" Gabriel asked doubtfully.

I swallowed hard. No, I wasn't sure at all. "I don't see any other option."

Avian's eyes met mine, and to my surprise, pride shone in them. He draped an arm across my shoulders. "Sounds like a plan." Hopefully gone were his days of overprotectiveness.

Avian's confidence bolstered mine.

Old habits dying hard, we all turned to Gabriel for approval.

He didn't respond at first. He eyed me carefully, his eyes unable to keep from drifting up to the scar that wrapped around my head. When his eyes met mine again, they were resolved. "Let's do it."

I nodded. "I want you guys to wait a ways back. Keep the hatch locked until I give the go ahead. If this doesn't work, I'm not risking any of you getting infected."

Avian hesitated, and finally nodded. "You're never going to change, are you?" he said, cracking a smile. "Always putting yourself in danger to save the rest of us."

"Never," I said, a smile tugging at my own lips.

We rolled the tank closer and Tuck parked. They wouldn't be able to see much from this far away but I came up with a signal to let them know when it was safe to come to the bridge.

As soon as they had the tank parked and I walked away from it, Bane started stepping out from their hiding places.

"You'll follow me," I said loudly. There were more and more of them emerging every second. My heart started hammering as there came to be twenty, fifty, seventy of them.

"You will not look away, you will go nowhere else," I said loudly again as I started walking toward the bridge. "You will follow me to the bridge."

The crowd that had started forming between me and the bridge parted as I moved forward. I glanced over my shoulder and saw that they were indeed following me.

Looking forward once more, I concentrated my thoughts. I imagined every Bane that must be in this city, in the entire bay area. I imagined them collecting on the bridge. I called to each of them in my head, screamed for them to come to me.

At first the movement was hard to make out. I squinted through the cold, pale light, trying to see all the way to the other side of the bridge. The land was shifting, or so it looked. Like a dark avalanche. An avalanche that started funneling itself to the massive rust colored bridge.

With my first step onto the bridge, I questioned our decision to cross it. The road was cracked and some of the gigantic steel cables that held the bridge up had rusted away and snapped. And I was about to flood it with thousands and thousands of bodies.

Sensing that my time was going to quickly disappear, I broke into a sprint across the bridge. A thundering of feet followed me. And a horde rushed at me from the other side.

The bridge rattled and shook. The cables groaned and a sharp snap sounded as one broke and fell over the side. The bridge jerked sharply as the cable dangled toward the water.

I froze when I finally reached the middle of the bridge. I looked back the way I'd come to see thousands of bodies filling the road behind me. I turned again to observe those that were coming.

There were men and women and, always the most disturbing, children. There were old men who had no teeth but gleaming bones that cut through their saggy skin. A child that couldn't be more than eighteen-months-old crawled down the road. Its human flesh had worn away to expose cybernetic bones. I couldn't look at it. It was too disturbing to imagine the horrifying looking thing as a human that had once been someone's darling baby.

I faced the crowd that had followed me onto the bridge. They all looked at me, their faces blank and waiting for orders.

There now had to be well over a hundred thousand Bane on the bridge. And they all waited for my command.

"Jump," I said, too quiet to be heard very far.

But every body turned to one side of the bridge or the other. They climbed the rail, balancing there for just a half a moment.

And then they jumped.

The water hissed as the cybernetics inside of them shorted out and died. Sparks of light flashed under the water and the bodies sank to the bottom of the ocean.

Come, I thought. *Meet a real end. Reclaim your humanity through death. Be released from this manmade hell. Go on to the afterlife you should have been allowed to earn.*

Bodies continued to flood onto the bridge. They crossed to the middle. Then they climbed the rail, and took the leap.

This went on for an hour.

I had no way of calculating how many of them jumped to their death, or whatever you call the end of a machine. But there had to have been nearly three hundred thousand of them. Maybe more.

I had reached them all.

They had all heard me.

And they had all obeyed.

There was something terrible and fearful about that kind of power. Something that made my hands shake and my stomach weak.

I was just Eve. I was just a girl who didn't understand people most of the time. I was just a girl who never said the right things.

I wasn't a girl who could control hundreds of thousands.

I wasn't this god of TorBane.

Finally, the last dozen bodies dropped into the water.

I turned to wave my arms in the air, to signal to the others that it was safe to cross. Then there was a pulsing, piercing pain behind my eyes. My head felt like it was splitting in two.

A scream ripped from my throat as I collapsed onto my knees. My hands came up to either side of my head and I pressed in, trying to keep my head from falling apart.

I opened my eyes but everything looked vividly green and numbers flashed across my vision. There were degree symbols and feet and inches. Something that looked like longitude and latitude.

Slowly it formed into a three-hundred eighty-one. The number flashed five times.

"Eve!" I faintly heard Avian scream.

And everything went black.

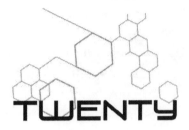

TWENTY

"You've got to wake her up, now!" a voice shouted. A gun fired.

I gasped for air as my eyes slid open. All four of the men were at the hatch. Another round of shots was fired. Something hit the side of the tank just as I jerked into a sitting position.

"Move!" I bellowed, grabbing the shotgun that was at my side. Bill and Tuck ducked back into the tank, providing a hole big enough at the hatch for me to pop out of.

There were probably twenty Bane rushing the tank.

I fired as I concentrated my thoughts.

The Bane turned on each other. One ripped another's arm clean off. Another broke his brother's neck. Another simply started beating another Bane to a crushed pile of metal and skin.

Avian, Gabriel, and I picked off the rest of them. Then the afternoon was still.

"What happened?" I asked as I took in our surroundings. We were on a narrow highway, the ocean directly to the west, a steep hillside with little more than shrubs covering it to the other side.

"We're just outside Santa Cruz," Bill said as we all dropped back inside and closed the hatch. "We were waiting for you to wake up before we went into the city, but there was a pack of Hunters."

"What about earlier?" I asked, trying to remember what had happened after the Bane had started jumping in the water.

There was nothing.

"We were about to come across the bridge when you collapsed," Avian said, concern in his eyes. "You screamed and then crumpled to the ground. You were unresponsive for over an hour."

"We didn't dare wait," Gabriel said. "We had no way to be sure you'd cleared all the Hunters out of the city, we had to get out of there. We're already behind schedule."

I nodded, closing my eyes. There was a dull throb behind them.

"What did they do to you?" Avian said quietly, pressing a kiss to my forehead.

"I think we need to hurry up," I said, swallowing hard. "I need to see Dr. Beeson."

We didn't stop.

We didn't take time to come up with elaborate plans to wipe out the Bane as we moved. I simply sat atop the tank and managed to keep the Bane back as we drove through city after city. I ignored my drooping eyelids when night came. If I slept, that meant we would have to stop and hide somewhere, and that meant we wouldn't reach New Eden in time to warn them about the beacon.

My companions took turns driving and we continued through the night.

The night was easier. There were still some of the Bane that held to their old rules of inactivity during the night.

Avian never left my side except to take his shift driving. I could feel the anticipation inside of him. He wanted to take me home, to go back our abnormal normal schedule. To return to our rooms in the hospital or our tent on the beach. But he remembered how I'd been on the edge of a nervous breakdown before I'd been taken. Going back to the city was going to bring me right back to that point.

"I love you, you know that, right?" I said in the dark. Avian's strong fingers linked through mine. His hand was getting cold in the dark winter night.

He looked over at me, and even though I didn't turn to look at him, I knew his eyes would be serious. "I know," he said.

"No matter what happens to me, just don't forget that."

"Eve," he said, his voice rising in uncertainty. "Dr. Beeson is going to fix this. We'll get you back. Whatever they did to you, we'll find a way to repair it. And he can reverse your last adjustment."

I nodded, even though I didn't necessarily believe it was true.

"We'll wait in the mountains where we hid everyone a few months ago," Avian said, squeezing my hand tighter. "Next to the lake?" I remembered. I'd only spent a few hours there, but I remembered. "I'll stay with you. The others will go get Dr. Beeson, he'll come back and we'll figure this thing out."

I nodded emptily once again.

"Hey," Avian said. "Don't give up on me. I have faith in you, in this. In mankind. Don't give up on yourself."

I finally met his eyes. I couldn't find any words to say, so instead I just looked back out into the dark.

Because it wasn't just the worry that the people from the Underground had done irreparable damage to me that was eating me away. It was that I could feel that dark, ugly feeling creeping back up inside of me as we rolled back toward the city. The depression was settling in again. The emotions that had started pushing me towards my break were coating my insides with blackness.

There was something wrong with me and I wasn't sure an adjustment from Dr. Beeson could fix it.

I needed away from the city, but the city was where I was needed.

Like Avian had said, I was never going to change. I would always do what was needed of me. I would protect my family. I would keep being Eve until being Eve killed me.

"We'll be back as soon as we can," Gabriel assured me. He stood in the hatch, about to duck back inside.

"Okay," I said, nodding.

We watched the tank drive away.

"Let's find some dinner," I said, not giving a moment for speeches that made me feel no better. I dropped Avian's hand and headed into the trees.

He knew there was something wrong. Avian knew how to read me better than I knew how to read myself most of the time. But he also knew when I didn't want to talk. When I just needed to go back to my old instincts and do what I was good at.

After being in the Redwoods, this forest seemed dehydrated and starved. These trees were small, more shrub like. They felt like sad impersonations.

A movement to the left caught my attention. There was a flash of orange and white. I crept behind a tree, peering around it.

A fox was eating something. Feathers. A bird.

Knowing my shotgun was going to riddle the body with buck shot, I opted for my knife instead. Well, Tristan's knife. Tristan's shotgun too.

I flicked my wrist and embedded the blade in the side of its neck. It gave a choked off howl before it collapsed to the ground.

Avian skinned it while I built a fire. My stomach actually started growling. It seemed like it had been ages since I'd had fresh meat.

I dared a glance at Avian while we ate. I wasn't really in the mood to talk but Avian almost always was. So his silence was out of place.

He stared into the fire, his expression distant. His shoulders were shrugged up towards his ears. He picked at his meat absentmindedly.

190

I knew he was trying to think of a way to fix the problem that was me. He was turning the situation over and over in his head, trying to find a way to keep me from going crazy. But we were both needed in the city.

Avian spent too much time worrying about me.

"I haven't forgotten about what you said the night of Victoria and Wix's wedding, you know," I said. I leaned over and bumped his shoulder with mine. "About wearing a white dress for you someday."

He looked over at me, the spark instantly back in his eyes. "Oh yeah?"

"Don't know how a girl could forget something like that." It was incredible how the air instantly lightened around us, the pressure lifting off my chest. "Sarah told me about marriage proposals once. I don't think you did it quite right."

Avian smiled, one that lit up his whole face. "I never said that was a proposal. I can be a little more grand than that. I was just asking you a question that night."

"You said, as we were looking at Victoria's wedding dress, 'would you wear one for me someday?' Did that not count?" I was smiling now, too.

"No it does not," Avian said as he leaned in closer, his nose only inches from mine. "Like I said, I can be a little more grand than that."

"You're going to build up expectations in my head, staying stuff like that," I said as I breathed in his nearness. "Are you sure you'll be able to live up to them?"

"Are you doubting me?" He brushed his lips against mine.

I met his eyes, that familiar hunger rising in my blood. His hand was hot on my cheek despite the cool around us. I was aware of every place his body touched mine. The way he breathed in and out touched a place in me that felt similar to the way my heart beat in my chest.

Then suddenly it felt like an arrow pierced me between the eyes.

I screamed out, crumpling into Avian's lap.

"Eve!" he yelled, pulling me close into him.

I opened my eyes, a vivid green wash and numbers flashing across my vision. I pressed my hands in on either side of my head.

"Ahh!" I screamed, feeling like my brain was going to explode.

"Stay with me, Eve!" Avian called to me from somewhere outside the pain.

A sixty-two point one pulsed across my vision and then everything was dark.

TWENTY-ONE

A blinding light suddenly filled my vision and I reacted on instinct.

My fist connected with a jaw.

Someone swore and I was momentarily blind as I climbed to my feet.

"That's probably the first time someone has ever punched you, isn't it Addie?"

I blinked furiously, trying to clear the white lights blocking my vision. "Royce?" I asked.

"Yeah, I'm here," he said.

Finally the white started to fade from my vision, leaving only the dull pain behind my eyes. Addie, Dr. Beeson's assistant, was pulling herself into a sitting position, cradling her reddened jaw. She gave me a disbelieving look. Royce laughed, shaking his head.

"That would indeed be the first time someone has ever punched me," Addie said as she picked herself up off the ground, brushing dirt from her clothes.

"I'm sorry," I said, shaking my head once more. "Instinct, I guess. Where's Dr. Beeson?"

"He's been really sick," Addie said. "Pneumonia. There's been a bad case of the flu at the hospital."

"Is he going to be okay?" I asked.

Addie shrugged. "Sounds like it. It's just going to take time. It seems like everyone is on the tail end of things."

"Do you remember what happened this time?" Avian asked, turning back to me. He eased me down onto a fallen tree. When the world swayed to the left a bit, I didn't fight him.

I shook my head. "Just pain all of the sudden. And then passing out. Just like before."

"And this is the second time this has happened since you were released?" Addie asked.

Avian took a small, silver cylinder from her and crouched in front of me. He pressed a button on the bottom and a tiny beam of light erupted from it. He shone it in my eyes, using his thumb to open them wider.

"I did this same thing two days ago," I said as I looked into the light.

"This isn't at all like before," Avian said as he stood, clicking the light off, and handing it back. "When she'd get emotionally overloaded and shut down. She was never in pain before."

"Well, she's not supposed to be feeling pain at all," Addie said. I stiffened momentarily. I wasn't particularly comfortable with her knowing all of my hybrid details. "Whatever is going on inside of her head must be pretty intense."

"What were they after?" Royce asked, always direct. "What did Margaret want from you?"

194

"They seemed the most interested in the reason why I don't spread the infection, why I can't be infected," I said, climbing to my feet as Royce pulled me upright. "I think they thought they might find a cure or something."

"Did they find it?" he asked, his interest piqued.

I shook my head. "I don't think so."

Royce nodded, his eyes drifting up to my new scars. "Bald is a good look on you," he said. He tried to keep a straight face, but I saw it crack, just slightly.

"Not funny, Royce," Avian scolded, glaring.

"Who says I'm joking?" he said, winking at me.

I just shook my head and lay back on the tree, blocking the sun with my hand. I felt out of sorts and violated. I was fifteen hundred miles away from the Underground and they were still torturing me somehow.

"Royce, we have to get the Pulse back up and ready," I said, looking up at him. "I'm assuming Gabriel told you what's going to happen?"

He nodded, his expression darkening. "Dr. Beeson's team is finishing up the energy storage devices. They'd started them just before you were taken. They'll get them wrapped up tonight and then get the Pulse prepped tomorrow."

I shook my head. "It doesn't just end with the beacon, Royce. Things are changing out there. The Bane, they really are getting smarter. They're sweeping through the country."

I recounted every horrifying detail I'd learned from Tom.

"They're going to come for us," I said, imagining how it would play out in my head. The buildings that would fall. How we would cower inside the hospital until they started ripping it apart one steel beam at a time. "We've got to fight back."

"Fighting back is what you and I do best. Let's get you home so we can figure out how."

"Royce, I can't go back into the city," I said, shaking my head. "If the Bane really are attracted to me, I could call them back into New Eden without even meaning to. And we have no idea what the Underground did to me. I won't put everyone at risk."

"I'm a little insulted that you doubt my abilities to protect our people," Royce said, actually looking offended. "We did survive in the city for five years before you wandered into town. We'll turn the wireless transmission system back on. If you do call them, we'll have it and the Pulse ready. We've always got bullets."

"You're sure I should come back?" I asked.

Royce nodded.

"We'll be able to do further testing back at the lab," Addie said. "There isn't much I can do out here with no equipment and no electricity."

Avian's hand rested on my shoulder and I turned to look at him. There was understanding in his eyes. He knew I didn't want to go back into the city. But he also saw the fire in me. It was time to fight back.

I turned back to Royce. "Let's go then."

The four of us hiked back down to the main road. Avian climbed into the driver's seat when Royce said he wanted to talk more. We headed back for the hospital.

"They all jumped?" Royce asked, looking at me like he might be able to see what was inside of me that had changed. "Hundreds of thousands of them?"

"Yes," I said. "They didn't hesitate."

He was quiet for a moment but his eyes never left mine. I could see the wheels turning in his head. Royce was one of the smartest men I knew. If anyone could figure out how to use my new ability to its full advantage, it would be him.

"Got anything?" I asked.

"Not yet," he said, breaking eye contact.

"Whoa," Avian suddenly said, grinding to a halt. "Did you guys feel that?"

"What?" Royce asked, leaning forward in his seat, his eyes sweeping the road and the buildings around us.

The ground shook and there was a great rumbling sound.

"That," Avian whispered.

The ground vibrated harder, the air filled with the sounds of the earth grinding and shifting.

"It's an earthquake," Addie said, her voice rising.

"Drive!" Royce shouted.

Avian slammed on the gas and we rocketed forward.

The truck shook back and forth violently and for a moment it tipped up on two wheels.

I looked out the window to see all the other abandoned vehicles outside shifting and rocking in place. The mostly dead palm trees swayed.

"Ever had an earthquake out here before?" Avian shouted above the din.

"We always get a few little ones every year," Addie shouted. "Nothing like this though."

The ground gave one last quake and finally, as we rounded the corner and came up to the hospital's underground garage, the earth stood still.

"Check that everyone is okay!" Royce bellowed to his men as soon as Avian stopped the truck.

We all ran for the stairwell and our footsteps reverberated off the walls. We burst into the main lobby and our ears were assaulted with shouting and screams.

There was glass all over the floor in the lobby where the computers had fallen and shattered. Papers were scattered everywhere. A screaming woman cowered under one of the desks, clutching her wrist which was bleeding profusely.

"I got her!" Avian shouted, breaking off and pulling off his shirt to press into the bleeding wound.

"Anyone else need medical attention?" Royce bellowed, pausing momentarily in the lobby. Everyone else seemed to be okay.

"Eve, take the second floor, find Elijah if you can. Make sure everyone is okay," Royce ordered. "Send everyone out the south doors. Addie, the blue floor."

We all broke off.

I dashed up the stairwell, taking them two at a time. They all seemed to be intact.

"Get off the stairs!" I shouted, dodging around a small group of older women cowering on a landing. "Royce wants everyone outside the building now! South entrance!"

They looked at me fearfully, but nodded and started down the stairs.

I stepped out into the hallway and started knocking on doors.

"Everyone alright in here?" I asked, finding a couple inside. There was stuff covering the floor, but nothing looked terribly damaged.

They nodded their heads. "You're back?"

"Yeah," I said, suddenly feeling self-conscious of my shaved head. "Royce wants everyone outside the south entrance."

They slipped into the stairway.

I continued to check doors. A woman had slipped in the shower when the quake started and hit her head on the sink. There was blood gushing from her eyebrow. I sent her in Avian's direction.

Elijah had worked his way down from the opposite end of the hallway and we met in the middle.

"Welcome back!" he shouted as the ground shook once more.

"Again?" I said, struggling to keep my balance.

"Aftershock," he said, waving me back toward the stairway. "They'll keep coming for a bit."

When we got to the stairway, we found a stampede of scientists in white lab coats frantically carrying equipment down the stairs. They shouted in angry, stressed voices. I made out words like "broken equipment" and "years of research".

The damage would be worst on the blue floor.

And my heart sank into my stomach.

"The Pulse," I said to Elijah, my eyes wide. "It's on the roof!"

"Don't worry," Elijah said as we waited for the scientists to clear out. "After those people took you, Royce had it moved to an underground, secure location."

"Is that going to be any better?" I asked as we descended the stairs.

"I don't know," he said, shaking his head. "Let's go check it out."

After we were sure everyone had made their way outside, we searched briefly for Royce to tell him where we were going. When he was nowhere to be found, we passed the message along to Avian as he stitched people up.

Elijah and I sprinted down the road. Another aftershock hit, nearly knocking us to the ground. He led me two blocks away and down into a parking garage.

There was a large steel door blocking off the entrance and Elijah pressed a number into a keypad. It beeped twice and retracted.

Dust billowed out at us as soon as the door started opening and Elijah swore loudly. We ducked beneath the door and Elijah shined a flashlight through the dust.

It looked like the back half of the building had collapsed down into the garage.

And one side of the Pulse was crushed completely.

Elijah swore again.

"It would have been perfectly safe from people like the ones that took you," Elijah said as we approached to inspect the damage. "Who would have anticipated that it would be Mother Earth that would turn on us this time?"

As we looked closer, it was only a quarter of the gigantic ring that had been smashed by a pillar that had toppled over on it.

"This took them four years to build," I said, panic building in my system. "We're going to have thousands and thousands of Bane falling on us in three days."

"So it's true?" Elijah asked, glaring at me through the dim light. "They really left a beacon here in the city?"

I nodded. "Come on," I said, turning and sprinting back outside.

We found Royce immediately when we got back to the hospital. The aftershocks seemed to have finally died out. He was barking for Elijah when we came up.

"The Pulse," I said, my voice anxious. "You've got to get it out of that garage. The entire building is about to collapse on it. It's already damaged."

Royce's face reddened further and he took half a moment to formulate a plan. "Get a team. Take one of the tanks. Pull it out of there!"

Elijah started shouting for his crew.

"You got this?" I asked Elijah, who nodded and headed for our own underground parking garage for one of the tanks.

I turned to see what I could do to help Royce when a bolt of lightning flashed through my brain and my knees buckled.

Everything illuminated in green. Numbers flashed everywhere. Suddenly they all pulsed and formed into a zero point one two in the center of my vision.

And the world was black again.

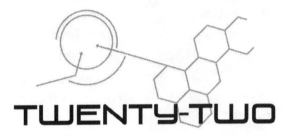

TWENTY-TWO

I was lying on a cot when I came to. It was dark and the air was cold.

I sat up and looked around.

It seemed everyone was sleeping outside. It must have been late, considering it looked like most everyone was in fact sleeping. Several small fires were scattered about, a few lone figures sat around them, warming their hands and talking.

I heard Avian speaking not far away and found him with Royce, their heads low, their voices heavy and quiet. I rose to join them.

They stood over a man and my entire body felt cold when his face and all of the blood came into view.

Eli. Morgan's husband. Expectant father.

"Is he…?" I tried to ask.

Avian met my eyes and nodded his head.

"What happened?"

"They were out with the rehoming crew," Royce said, his voice rough. "They were all cleaning a new building when the quake hit. The roof collapsed on them."

"He bled out," Avian said, his voice catching.

I squeezed my eyes closed, shaking my head.

"Where is Morgan?" I asked.

Avian pointed to a cot a ways away. She was curled into a ball around her slowly growing stomach. "She was hit too. It knocked her unconscious. She hasn't woken up yet."

"The baby?"

"We don't know."

I nodded, hugging my arms around me. "Will it be safe to go back inside the hospital?" I asked Royce. I couldn't dwell on the death and despair any more.

"Elijah's crew scouted it out. Everything looks okay," Royce said. "We want to check it again in the morning. We thought it safest to give everything some time to settle."

"Do you remember anything this time?" Avian asked me, walking around Eli's cot, pulling me into his arms.

I shook my head. "Same as the last two times."

"Once we get this all cleaned up Dr. Beeson will fix it," Avian said, pressing his forehead to mine. "It looks like most of the equipment made it through. He'll do what he does best."

I nodded, biting my upper lip. I suddenly recalled the memories and nightmares I'd had in the Underground, the dreams. Dr. Beeson evaluating me and declaring I didn't need an adjustment yet.

"Get some rest you two," Royce said as he covered Eli with a blanket. "There isn't much more you can do until morning."

"What about you?" I asked Royce. There were dark bags beneath his eyes.

"Not now," he said, shaking his head. "There will be no sleep for me tonight."

I wanted to ask him more questions. I wanted to know if we'd be able to fix the Pulse. We needed to make plans. I wanted to know if everyone else had made it out of the hospital okay. But his eyes told me he was done with questions for the night.

"Come on," Avian said, taking my hand and pulling me toward one of the fires.

We stopped in the firelight. Avian held his hands up to the flames to warm them. They were covered in blood.

"I'm going to try and go back to the tent tomorrow as soon as I can manage," I said, a lump in my throat. "I'm going to need some of my stuff."

Avian met my eyes with sadness. "When you're this close to the coast and there's an earthquake, often times the shore gets flooded. We're lucky a tsunami didn't rush in on us. There's a good chance the tent isn't there anymore."

I squeezed my eyelids closed, my stomach feeling sick. There was nothing in it that was dire, nothing that I couldn't find in this city elsewhere. Except for the picture of my mother.

"We'll check though," Avian said. He placed a finger on my chin. I opened my eyes to meet his. "It might still be there."

I could only nod once again.

I didn't sleep that night. Avian and I curled into each other on a blanket on the ground, never once letting go.

While I listened to his steady breathing, I could only gaze out into the dark night.

My thoughts turned to West. I wondered if he was okay. Would Margaret hurt him? Turn him out onto the Bane-infested streets?

I could only pray that Tristan would be able to protect West like he promised.

But would West even want to come back with Tristan? He'd left New Eden willingly to try and get away from me. How was he really supposed to move on if he had to see Avian and me every day? I wouldn't really be able to blame him if he didn't want to come back.

Finally morning started growing in the horizon. I pressed a kiss to Avian's forehead and went to see how I could help.

Avian's patients slept, probably with the aid of some kind of medication. Morgan was still sleeping, her eyes moving rapidly beneath her eyelids. While I certainly didn't want her to die, I almost wished for her to never have to wake up and find the love of her life and the father of her unborn child gone.

I was looking at Eli's empty cot when Gabriel stopped silently at my side. I observed his face, saw the heavy bags beneath his eyes. He'd been up most of the night, if not all of it. I had little doubt it had been him that had buried Eli.

"It's not fair," I said, looking back to the cot. It was covered mostly with a blanket, but it had slipped off one corner, exposing the blood stains. "He survived the Bane this long. And then to be killed by a force of nature?"

Gabriel cleared his throat and swallowed heavily. "No it isn't fair, but in a way it was a kind of beautiful way to die. Better to be claimed by nature than to be stolen by TorBane."

"I suppose."

By now the morning light had broken over the tops of buildings, calling everyone to wakefulness. I turned to see Avian roll over, his eyes searching the crowd. When he found me, a smile lit up his sleepy face.

This time I did manage to smile back.

Something moved in the corner of my eye. I looked over to see two figures down the street, moving slowly, struggling.

I took a few steps closer, squinting to see through the blinding sunlight.

"Tristan?" I said.

He looked up as I said his name. Then he and the figure at his side collapsed to the ground.

"West!"

I rushed toward them, at the same time Elijah, Nick, and Tuck did with guns pointed in their direction.

"No!" I shouted to them, waving a hand at them. "It's okay. He's a friend."

West was laying on the ground, looking totally out of it, his eyes dully searching the sky. He looked like he'd dropped fifteen pounds since I had last seen him. But the inhibitor was gone.

Tristan knelt on the ground next to him, his body trembling slightly in fatigue.

"Is he okay?" I asked Tristan, kneeling at West's side. I was conflicted, wanting to both assure myself that he was alive and wanting to strangle him at the same time for betraying me.

"He'll be fine," Tristan said. "He's actually drugged right now. I told him the truth about what happened with you and he was totally freaking out. I didn't want him getting too worked up during the journey until he could see that you were okay."

"Eve?" West mumbled, his eyes still totally unfocused. He blinked hard and shook his head.

"How did you get down here?" I asked, turning to Tristan and standing. "Surely you didn't walk this whole way."

He shook his head, a smile playing on his lips. "We took a boat. I didn't think we'd survive the drive down."

West moaned as he pulled himself into a sitting position. "My head," he said, pressing his hands into the sides of his head. "What did you give me?"

"A sedative," Tristan said with a chuckle. "It was intended for livestock, but it did the trick."

West finally opened his eyes, and saw me standing there with a hard expression. "Eve," he said, his voice rising as he made his way to his feet. "Eve, you've got to listen to me—"

And then Avian plowed into him.

They both skidded across the concrete and hadn't even stopped before Avian's fists were connecting with West's jaw.

"You've screwed Eve over for the last time!" Avian screamed. "And now you've probably killed us all!"

"Avian!" I screamed, lunging after him at the same time Nick did.

Avian shoved me off and punched Nick. He turned back to West and to my horror, pulled his hand gun and leveled it in West's face.

"You keep making mistake after mistake," Avian whispered. "And I am sorry for what you've gone through, but I'm getting tired of forgiving you. This...what you did to her this time...I'm not letting this go."

"Avian!" I yelled again, taking a slow step forward. "This isn't you. You don't want to hurt him."

"Believe me," Avian said, shaking his head, his eyes never leaving West's. "I do."

"Avian, I—" West started.

"Shut up!" Avian screamed, spit flying from his mouth. He shoved his gun in West's face again. "You don't deserve any more second chances. I nearly lost her forever because of you!"

"Avian, don't do this," I said as I took another step toward him.

I looked up to Nick, who met my worried gaze for a second. I saw the action in his eyes before I could yell to stop him.

Nick rushed forward. His arms wrapped around Avian's waist and they both rolled over the concrete, wrestling for the gun.

A shot fired.

Nick collapsed to the road, his breath's coming in shallow gasps. His hands clutched his bleeding abdomen.

"Nick!" I screamed, darting forward to press my own hands into his to try and stop the blood.

"No," Avian whispered. "I didn't... I'm sorry... I—"

Elijah tackled Avian, forcing his face to the ground. He snapped a pair of handcuffs around Avian's wrists.

"Royce!" Elijah bellowed. "Dr. Sun!"

The next sixty seconds were a blur of Avian apologizing, his eyes wild, Royce barking for Avian to be taken into confinement, men hauling the bleeding Nick and West back to the hospital, and Tristan and I standing there stunned, not knowing what had just happened or what to do.

They all shut me out.

Elijah locked Avian up and he, Royce, Gabriel, and everyone else important headed for the conference room to figure out a plan. As well as what to do with Avian.

They literally locked me out.

"Eve," Tristan said. He'd followed me up to the sixth floor and we both stood outside the locked door. "I really need to talk to you."

It took me a long moment to respond. I just stood staring at that locked door thinking I should be inside, helping to formulate a plan for how to save everyone here.

The Pulse was broken, and we had less than seventy-two hours until the Underground set off their hidden beacon.

And Avian was locked up like a criminal.

I had to do something. But what?

"Eve?" Tristan repeated.

"Okay," I finally said.

I led him down into my room and locked the door behind me.

Out of view of everyone else, Tristan suddenly engulfed me in a hug. "You made it back okay then?"

"Yeah," I answered, surprised at his bold move of affection. I patted his back awkwardly before he released me.

"I have to admit, I was worried I was sending you away to get ripped apart," he said, his eyes dark. "Things started getting worse at the Underground after you left."

"More break-ins?" I asked, my stomach hollowing out.

"Twice," he nodded, his eyes turning to the window and the streets outside, like he didn't quite believe that the city was actually cleared. "We got it the first time before anything happened. But we lost a soldier the second time."

"I'm sorry," I said. I truly was, despite what they had done to me. "Are you okay? Did they punish you after you let me go?"

This was when his eyes truly darkened. "That's what I needed to talk to you about. They never questioned anyone after they discovered you were gone. But I kept getting all these knowing looks. They knew it was me, Eve. But they never said a word. They acted like they expected this, like they might have even planned your escape."

I was quiet for a moment, digesting what this would possibly mean. "They wanted me to get out of there."

Tristan nodded. "And I think they wanted you to get back quickly. Those were Alistar's keys I took. To his motorcycle. I didn't think about it at the time, but I found them just outside my door. They looked like they had been dropped there by accident. But I don't think it was any mistake. I don't think Margaret is quite finished with you, Eve."

My blood turned cold as I met Tristan's eyes again. A shaky hand rose to my head, running along my scalp. There was now very short fuzz covering my skin. "Something has been happening," I whispered. "I keep having these head-splitting headaches. Blackouts that follow."

"I have little doubt that it is because of them," he shook his head. "Something is going to happen."

"Margaret was obsessed with the Pulse," I said. "I guarantee this has something to do with it."

"That's what cleared the city for you?" he asked.

I nodded. "She was livid when we told her we wouldn't use it when she was down here those few weeks ago. She's trying to force us to use it."

"I suggest you tell your people to have it ready." His eyes were dark and serious and regretful.

I shook my head this time, my eyes falling to the ground. "You just missed the earthquake. They hid the Pulse after the Underground took me. But it got damaged. There's no way it will work. And I have no idea how long it will take to fix."

Tristan swore under his breath.

All the information I'd learned, all the secrets and lies tumbled through my head, as if on repeat.

"Tristan," I whispered, my blood going cold. I froze, my gaze locking with his. "What if I'm the trigger?"

His face blanched. I could see the gears swirling in his head as things started to fall into place. "That's the reason they wanted you to escape."

"They put the trigger in my head and sent me back. What if I've already started some kind of countdown?"

"Then we're all in for a load of trouble," Tristan said in a low growl.

"Come on," I said, darting for the door. "We've got to tell Royce and Gabriel."

The two of us sprinted back to the staircase. We exploded onto the sixth floor and I started pounding on the door to the conference room.

"Royce!" I bellowed. "I have to talk to you *now* or we're all going to be dead!"

The door was yanked open and Royce's expression was livid. "I do not have time to deal with your love mess, Eve," he hissed in my face. "Avian shot someone, I can't ignore…"

"I think I'm the trigger," I interrupted him, pushing my way past him into the room. "I'm going to set the beacon off, if I haven't already set off some kind of countdown."

Everyone in the room finally froze and every gaze locked on me.

"This is Tristan," I said, holding a hand out toward him where he stood just outside the door. I waved him in. "He was the one who helped me escape and brought West back. He has something you need to hear."

I had to respect Tristan. There was no hesitation or intimidation in him. He launched into the story he'd told me. How this had all been a set up.

"It makes sense," I said, shaking my head when Tristan was done. "These blackouts I've been having, they have to have something to do with them. They wanted me to get home and get home quickly."

"I'd say let's put you on an ATV and get you far away from here, but what if you've already initiated a countdown?" Elijah said.

"We have to evacuate the city," Royce growled, glaring at me. "With how much smarter and more aggressive the Hunters have gotten, the wireless transmission system might not be enough to keep them out of the hospital. Even if it is on lockdown."

"The water," Tristan said, his hands on his hips. "Most of the Bane won't even get near it. You head out into the water and you'll be safe."

"We can't just abandon the hospital though," Gabriel said, his brow furrowing. "We'll survive out on the water for a while, but we're going to have to come back to land. We have to get the Pulse back up and running and that's not going to happen if we're all hiding on a ship off the coast."

"Thank you for your information, Eve," Royce said, again glowering at me. He placed a hand on both of my shoulders and maneuvered me toward the door.

"Wait a second—" I started fighting.

"You've caused enough trouble for one day," he said, shoving me toward the door and then pushing Tristan towards it as well. "Leave the plotting to the grown-ups."

He closed the door in our faces.

"Royce!" I yelled, pounding on the door. "Gabriel!"

No one replied.

"Eve," a voice called down from the hall. I turned to see Bill, marching toward us with a shotgun in hand. "Leave them alone. Never thought I'd be called for backup with you as a threat."

"You're here because of me?" I said, my voice livid.

"Elijah radioed me up to escort you away from this floor," he said, regret in his eyes.

I shook my head, clenching my jaw. "I assume you've heard about all the drama?" I asked as I reluctantly walked away from the door, Tristan in our wake.

Bill nodded.

"Any idea how Nick is doing?" I asked.

"He's in surgery," Bill said, shaking his head. "It doesn't look very good."

I swore under my breath, closing my eyes for a moment.

"Avian really freaked out like that?" Bill asked, the disbelief obvious in his voice.

It took me a moment to nod. The whole scene hadn't seemed real. "Avian's never been a violent person. Never."

"I assume that's the guy you're involved with?" Tristan asked.

"Yeah," I responded as we entered the stairway. "Any idea what they're going to do with him?"

Bill shook his head. "Royce has him locked up on the fourth floor for now. He said something about determining his fate when we learn Nick's."

I swallowed hard. What had Avian been thinking?

"What about West?" I asked as we descended the stairs.

"He's in the hospital wing right now," Bill responded as we exited on the main level. "Avian banged him up pretty bad, but Dr. Stone is patching him up."

I swore again as we paused in the lobby. "Can anything else go wrong?"

"Knock on wood," Tristan said, shaking his head. "Are things always so dramatic around here?"

A chuckle unexpectedly erupted from my lips and I shook my head. "No kidding."

"Now, are you going to cause any more issues, or can I go back to work?" Bill asked.

"I make no promises," I answered honestly.

Bill just shook his head with a hint of a smile and walked away.

"Well, this was quite the introduction to your little colony," Tristan said as his eyes swept the lobby.

"Welcome to New Eden."

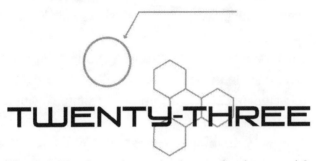

TWENTY-THREE

What could I do at that point but go back to work?

I'd tried to demand to see Avian, but Raj, who stood guard outside his door, refused me in a very in-my-face kind of way. He literally shoved his rifle in my face and told me I wasn't allowed to talk to Avian.

I had no control. I couldn't dig the remote out of my head, if there was one. I couldn't make Royce figure out a plan any faster. I couldn't make them all come out of that room. I couldn't decide Avian's fate. I couldn't save Nick.

But I could work.

Tristan and I helped move everyone back into the hospital when it was determined safe. No one was to go back to their houses except to get supplies until we knew what to do.

Besides the Pulse, nothing major had been damaged during the earthquake.

I gave Tristan the tour of the hospital as people started settling down. He marveled over the kitchens, over the lobby, over the school rooms. I couldn't blame him. It was

216

the same reaction I had the first time Royce had shown us around.

"Do you think you'll stay?" I asked him as we sat in the dining area, eating dinner. "Here in New Eden?"

Tristan met my eyes for a moment before dropping them to his plate again. "I don't think I could go back," he said, pushing his eggs around on his plate. "I can just feel it here. How different things are, despite your drama. I hope you appreciate how unique of a situation you have here, these good people. The fact that you all work together in harmony."

I nodded as I finished off my roll. "I haven't been anywhere but with these people since the Evolution, but I know we're lucky."

"So to answer your question, yes, if New Eden will have me, I'd like to stay," Tristan said.

"You helped me get home," I said with a smile. "If you were looking for immediate acceptance, that pretty much guaranteed it. I know everyone is kind of pissed at me right know, but we're all still family."

Tristan chuckled, looking back at me. "I think they're happy to have you home for more than the reason of being family. You're probably still the key to fixing all this somehow. How does it not go to your head, being so blasted important?"

"Oh, the knowledge that I helped bring about the end of the world keeps me pretty humble," I said, my tone sarcastic.

"Good point," Tristan said, his tone teasing and serious at the same time.

"What about you?" I asked, stacking my empty plate on his. "Where were you when everything fell apart?"

"Well," he said, sitting back in his chair and crossing his arms over his chest. "I was sixteen. I was in high school and my best friend told me how his cousin had been acting weird after her surgery. She was a first gen. A few days later I heard something on the news about TorBane spreading and a week later, my best friend wasn't human any more. As soon as I told my dad about it, he took us into the mountains."

"How did you end up in Seattle then?" I asked, folding my arms on the table and leaning forward.

"My dad went out on a hunting trip one day, looking for some food for us. I was seventeen then. I was supposed to watch our camp because there had been marauders in the area. Dad never came back."

"I'm sorry to hear that," I said, truly meaning it.

Tristan gave a little nod with a tight-lipped smile in appreciation. "There was this man, Stanley, who found me. He didn't say much, but he said I could come with him, that he'd try his best to keep the both of us safe. Eventually we ended up at the Underground. Eventually he ended up getting infected."

I shook my head. "There are so few of us left."

"Eve?" a voice called from behind. I turned to see Lin rushing across the room.

She collided with me as she skidded across the tile floor, engulfing me in a hug. "I heard you were back. Are you okay?" She backed away slightly, her eyes instantly going to my shaven head and the scars there.

"I don't know about okay," I said. "But I'm back."

"Your hair," she said, her face falling. "You always had the most beautiful hair. That doesn't hurt, does it?" She gingerly touched the scars.

"I'm a freak, remember?" I teased her with serious eyes.

"Ah, yes, no pain," she said. "And who is this?"

"Lin, this is Tristan," I said, turning back to him. "Tristan, this is my…friend, Lin."

And suddenly I felt like I had taken advantage of Lin. I knew she would have called me a friend without a second thought. I sometimes needed to remember people were people, not just tools for survival.

"Nice to meet you, Lin," Tristan said, extending a hand toward her. He held a mischievous smile on his face.

"And you too," Lin said. Lin smiled a lot, but this one was different.

I'd never been a matchmaker before.

I had to hope then that we'd all live long enough for them to get to know each other.

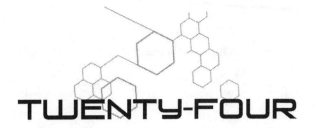

TWENTY-FOUR

The plan was this:

In forty-eight hours the vast majority of New Eden would evacuate the hospital. They would pack their necessities and head for the harbors and everyone would take off into the water. Special teams would pack as much food and provisions as possible in those forty-eight. They would all have roughly eight hours to get to safety.

I would stay at the hospital as well as a handful of the scientists while they repaired the Pulse. We would have the wireless transmission system on full blast and would keep the hospital on lock down, just how they'd all survived before the Pulse went off. Royce would stay with us and Gabriel would go with everyone else to the water.

And we'd work as fast and furious as we could to rid the city once again of the Bane that were about to be called out.

Because no one saw a solution to stopping the beacon.

While everyone else prepared for evacuation, I had a few personal issues to take care of.

Despite the panic that was sweeping the hospital and city about having to evacuate, there was endless talk.

People didn't know what to think about Avian's actions.

Some called for his immediate exile from New Eden. Violence against our own couldn't be tolerated. Could Avian be trusted anymore? What other ways would he lash out violently in the future?

Nick was still alive, but he only had a fifty-fifty chance of making it.

West had recovered from his injuries and had been released to prepare for evacuation. I made sure to avoid him. At this point it seemed best.

But I had to talk to Avian.

The floor was silent when I stepped out from the stairway. The lights on this floor flickered, air rushed through the vents, giving the feeling there where whispering ghosts whispering. Waiting to tell you their secrets.

I moved silently through the hall, finding it empty. Glancing around the corner, I spotted Raj, slumped on the floor. I could faintly hear his snore.

There was a supply closet just to the left of where he slept. I grabbed an electrical cord that was lying on the floor next to me and silently crept forward.

In one swift movement, I yanked his rifle from his hands and threw it down the hall. With my other hand, I grasped the front of his shirt and hauled him up and into the closet. He gave a startled, half-asleep yell, but he was too disoriented to fight back. I stuffed him into the closet and pulled the door closed. I wound one end of the chord around the handle and then wound the other end around a door handle across the hall.

The door to the closet jerked, but the cord held, locking Raj inside.

"Eve!" he yelled, his voice faint through the solid door. "Don't do this! These are Royce's orders!"

"I just need to talk to him," I said, though probably not loud enough for him to hear me.

I turned to the door he'd been guarding. It looked like any normal hospital room, but it locked from the outside. I wondered if Royce had ordered it special made for Avian or if he'd thought to have a prison room before everything went down.

"Avian?" I called, knocking on the door.

"Eve?" he responded. I heard his feet shuffled across the floor. "Is that you?"

"Yeah," I said, my voice rough. I'd tried to rehearse what I would say to him when I faced him once more, but nothing had come. "I'm coming in. Stand back from the door."

He shuffled away and I set my own shotgun down for a moment. Coiling my right leg back, I landed a solid blow next to the door handle. The wood split but not enough to open the door. On the third kick, it caved and flew open.

Avian stood in the middle of the room. He had dark circles under his eyes and his entire countenance seemed darker.

But the grief and pain on his face showed me that he was still Avian.

"I'm sorry," he said, the words cracking.

"I know," I said. But I didn't move farther into the room.

222

"I don't know what came over me," he said. His eyes dropping to the floor. He shook his head. I'd never seen his hair so long. He was probably going on a month without a shave. "I just kept thinking about how you could have died when they had you cut open and how we were all going to get infected because of what he'd done. I didn't mean to hurt anyone."

"I know," I said, the words sticking in my throat.

"I don't expect you to forgive me for what I did, Eve," he said, his gaze finally rising to meet mine. "I don't expect you to love a monster."

"We're all monsters in some way or another."

Avian held my eyes for a long time and moisture brimmed in his. He gave a small nod.

"What is Royce planning to do with you?" I asked as I slid my hands into my pockets. I couldn't make myself move into the room.

"I don't think he has time to figure that out with the impending evacuation," he said. "But I'm not going to be one of the evacuees."

My throat felt tight and the words I tried to say couldn't move up my throat.

"Eve," he breathed and took two steps forward.

"Promise me you'll never do something like that again," I forced out, my words louder and more broken sounding than I had intended them to be. "Promise me you will never hurt one of us, ever again. Because that man back there, I don't know who he was."

Avian froze, and his face became all the whiter. He swallowed hard. "It was unforgivable. I don't know who

223

that man was either. And I *promise*, you will never, *ever,* see him again."

I nodded, trying to push the knot in my throat down. "Good. Because I need you right now. Always."

I didn't hold back any longer. I rushed forward, crushing myself into his chest.

"I forgive you," I said into the fabric of his shirt. "As long as you never do anything stupid like that again."

"Promise," he whispered into my short, fuzzy hair. He kissed the top of my head.

"After everyone is evacuated, I'll talk to Royce about your release," I said, looking up at him. "Once everything begins, I'm sure we'll need you."

"Whatever everyone thinks is suitable punishment, I'll take it," he said, his voice dead sounding. "I deserve it."

"You're human, Avian. We all make mistakes."

I knocked on the thick black door of Dr. Beeson's office. After ten seconds it opened.

It was Addie who answered.

"How's Dr. Beeson doing?" I asked. Addie held the door open just wide enough for her face to pop out.

"He's still pretty out of it," she said, her entire demeanor crest fallen. I understood it. Dr. Beeson, helping him with his research and work, it was her entire world. "Dr. Stone has him all drugged up but he thinks Erik will be okay by the time everything goes down."

I nodded, my eyes falling to the floor. I shifted from one foot to the other. My heart started beating quicker.

"Are you okay?" she asked, her eyes narrowing.

There was no hesitation when I shook my head. "This last adjustment, it was too much," I said. I finally looked up. "I need him to fix me."

Addie's eyes darted back into the office before looking back at me.

"He said something about that in his notes," she said.

I was a little annoyed that she had access to nearly everything in Dr. Beeson's office, including such detailed notes about me. That felt too personal. I would have rather kept it between the two of us. We had history, history that didn't need to be shared with anyone in the present.

"I am very familiar with the wireless transmission system," Addie said. She fidgeted. "I helped him develop it. He trained me extensively. I was the one who got it back up and running yesterday. He always said that should something happen to him, someone would need to know how to work it. I've read all the notes on what he does with your adjustments. I'm ninety-five percent confident I could do it. If you'd like."

Addie's offer threw me. It took a lot of trust to let Dr. Beeson mess with my head. He could do anything to me when I was shut down and vulnerable like that. He could turn me into a blithering idiot. He could turn me back into an infant. But I trusted him to help me.

Could I trust Addie?

"I promise I won't do anything other than restore your emotional blockers," Addie said, as if she could read my mind. "Trust me, I have no interest in harming you. You're pretty much the most amazing science experiment I've ever met."

My eyes must have darkened because she apologized.

"What I mean is that I will make sure it works," she said. "I promise."

This seemed stupid. I knew if Avian was here there was no way he would allow me to do this. Nearly anyone in the hospital would protest.

But that beacon was about to go off. The Underground wasn't finished with me and I needed to be at the top of my game if I was going to fight back.

"Promise?" I asked. "You're sure you can do this?"

"Ninety-five percent," Addie said, giving a little nod.

"That's going to have to be sure enough, I guess."

She opened the door wider and let me in.

The air was crisp with the promise of the New Year. I rolled Avian's motorcycle out of the underground garage. I was clouded in exhaust fumes as I started the engine.

I took a solid breath before I started down the road.

I finally felt like me again.

I didn't feel like I was going to crack at any moment, like I was going to have a meltdown. I could see things clearly and my insides didn't feel like a snaking mess.

Addie had done the adjustment perfectly.

Even though my emotions were dulled back to normal, there was something very personal I had to investigate for myself before I got down to Bane business.

One moment I had myself convinced that there was no way my tent could be washed away, the next I couldn't image that it hadn't been.

But when I parked the motorcycle next to the beach, I saw it, sitting battered and sideways, but still there.

My boots sank into the wet sand. The shoreline looked different, as if the water had in fact rushed in, dragging the granules away. The tide had pulled my tent down the beach. It sat only two feet from the water.

I righted two of the poles before I stepped inside.

The floor was soggy and my clothes that had been stashed under the cot were soaked. But when I checked underneath my pillow, I found the picture of my mother, undamaged.

I held it to my chest, taking a deep breath.

My past.

Had I been remembering it back at the Underground? Were those scenes and images real? Or had I just been going crazy? Had they broken my brain enough to make me see things that just mimicked reality?

I looked down at the woman who looked just like me.

If she hadn't died giving birth to me, the world might still be recognizable. She might have stopped Dr. Evans from giving me TorBane, let me die the natural death I should have died, and TorBane might have just stayed a theory in a file.

But these thoughts weren't going to change the past. So I put them away.

Tucking the picture in my pocket, I rescued a few of Avian's books and tucked them into my pack.

I took my time emptying the tent. I broke into one of the houses that sat on the beach, storing my clothing, cot, pillow, sleeping things, Avian's belongings, and eventually, the tent, inside.

I was doomed to live forever inside prison walls.

When I was finished, I stood with the tips of my boots in the water. I closed my eyes, breathing the ocean air in. Before me was freedom and peace. At my back was the real world of destruction and endless, crushing work.

"Goodbye," I whispered to the water as my eyes opened. I knew that it would be a while before I would see it again.

Straddling the bike, I pointed it back in the direction of the hospital.

I wove between bodies that lay on the streets, all Hunters that had been outside when the Pulse had gone off. It seemed unreal that that had only been three months ago. So much had happened since then.

I was three blocks from the hospital when something caught my eye.

A movement. Something darting behind a building.

I stopped the motorcycle on the side of the road and killed the engine. I pulled my Desert Eagle from my back pocket. Peeking around the corner, I slipped silently along the wall.

My handgun was held steady when I popped around the corner, only to find an empty alley.

Something hit my shoulder—dirt—and my eyes jumped up just in time to see a foot disappearing over the edge of the roof.

I scaled the fire escape, making sure my feet were silent as I did. And just as I got onto the roof, I saw two figures jump off the side of the building.

I sprinted across the roof. Bodies hit something solid with a clatter and a curse below me and then feet were running.

I looked over the side of the roof just as they disappeared around a corner.

Darting back to the fire escape, I slid down the ladder and ran back to the motorcycle. I pushed it to close to eighty miles an hour in the three blocks I had left.

When I rounded the final corner, I saw a crowd of people in front of the main entrance of the hospital and stopped the bike on the grass there.

Elijah had his foot on the back of a man who was handcuffed and on his knees. Graye held a gun to the man's head. Royce stood before him, his arms crossed over his chest.

"What's going on?" I asked, joining them.

"Graye found him spying about fifteen minutes ago," Elijah said. "He's not saying what he's doing or where he's from."

"I highly suggest you start talking," Royce said, squatting right in front of the man. "You see, when I worked for the United States government developing weapons of war, I got a contract to develop a few nasty items for a more individual base of destruction. You do not want me digging in my closet. But I will if you don't tell me what I want to hear."

Fear shook the man's body, but he was trying hard to keep his face blank.

"Is it ready?" he asked, his voice shaking slightly.

"Is what ready?" Royce asked, narrowing his eyes at him.

"The device."

"What…the Pulse?"

The man nodded.

"You're with them," Royce said, his eyes growing even darker. "Aren't you? You're with that group from Seattle."

Tristan stepped out of the hospital and hesitantly came to my side. "What's going on?" he asked.

"Apparently your old friends are back." I took a step forward. "There were more of them just a few blocks from—"

My head must have split open for real this time.

A scream ripped from my throat and I collapsed to my hands and knees. I was sure there had to be blood leaking from my ears and nose and eyes and mouth and every pore in my body. My brain was dissolving into a trillion atoms being split and rearranged.

I opened my eyes to find a world washed in green, sequences of numbers flashing across my vision.

And I could feel them. Hundreds of thousands of them. Millions maybe. Like a string was connected to me and ran to each and every one of them.

I could feel the Bane.

And the call that was going from me to them.

"Eve!" voices screamed. My eyes searched for faces to attach the voices to. But there was only green and numbers and the feeling that I was more Bane in that moment than I had ever been in my life.

The connections became stronger and stronger and I felt their dire need, their drive, their one reason for existence—to make the perfection spread. To heal what was broken. And what was broken was human DNA and tissue. It was weak. It aged. It died. It fractured.

We were strong. We were perfect. We were made to save.

And we had to spread.

We had to make the world perfect.

"Eve!" a voice called out to me again.

I blinked, trying to clear the numbers from my vision and the voices from my head.

We must spread.

We must perfect and heal the world.

"Eve! This isn't you!" the voice screamed again.

Another voice yelled. And then a gun was fired.

I blinked again and my head jerked to the right as someone slapped me. It felt like a fishing hook caught in my brain and the strings that bound me to the millions out there started breaking away.

"Eve! Come on, you can pull out of this!"

Tristan.

"Tristan?" I moaned, the pain pulsing through my brain once again. I opened my eyes, the numbers fading from my vision as the rest of the strings fell away.

"I'm right here," he said. His arms were around me and I was lying on his lap. "Holy sh... You were saying some pretty freaky stuff."

And suddenly adrenaline burned through my veins. I was on my feet and ready to attack the man we had captured when I froze.

There had to be fifteen of the people from the Underground surrounding us. Guns were pulled everywhere. Elijah's team had assembled. And there was a body in the middle of us all.

"You put the beacon in my head, didn't you?" I growled at none of them in particular. "It was never here and I was never the trigger. You put it *in me* and sent me back!"

Most of them didn't react in any way, but one of them had a tiny smile that tugged on his mouth.

I crossed the circle faster than I'd ever moved. I yanked the shotgun from his hands and tossed it towards Tristan. I grabbed the man's shirt in my fist and pulled his face an inch from mine.

"You've just sentenced everyone to infection," I hissed.

"That's what the Pulse is for," he said, his breath rancid.

"The Pulse is broken!" I bellowed, shoving him away from me, knocking him to the ground. "And you set the beacon off two days early!"

"You put the beacon in one of our soldiers?!" Royce bellowed, rushing at one of the other men, knocking him to the ground, his fist crushing his cheekbone. Within half a second everyone was yelling, fists flying.

I had just knocked one of the men out who rushed me when I saw movement from behind us.

There were more of them.

Another ten soldiers, men and women, rushed from behind other buildings, guns drawn.

This was about to turn into a blood bath.

We didn't have to wait for the Bane to swarm the city in the next few hours. We were going to kill each other off first.

Graye chased after two soldiers who fled down an alley.

Tristan stood with one of our soldiers, trying to keep them out of the hospital, guns drawn.

Elijah radioed for back up as he fought off another man.

I had to find Margaret. If I could find Margaret, maybe I could keep this from turning into a death match. I could convince her to call off her people.

Because I had no doubt that Margaret was here.

Tristan was right. They had staged my escape. They'd wanted me to get back to New Eden and quickly.

Because when they didn't find the answer to curing TorBane, they planted their beacon inside of my head and waited for me to return. And then they set it off.

Looking one last time back at my family, I set off down the street.

TWENTY-FIVE

Margaret would be waiting somewhere she could see all the action. I just had to find her vantage point.

I checked the street level, anywhere she would be able to see from. But she wasn't a stupid woman and being out on the road would be too obvious. She was hiding inside a building.

I was just about to duck inside one when a familiar voice called my name.

I turned left and found West jogging up to my side. His entire body was bruised.

"We're going to kill each other off out there," he said, his eyes wild and fearful. He grabbed my arm and pulled me out of view of the battle.

I hadn't considered how I would react to West when I came face to face with him again after what he'd done, after what Avian had done. Especially since Addie had turned my humanity down.

I should have expected the hatred and the burning that consumed me.

And he saw it all there in my face.

234

"I am so sorry," he said, his eyes filling with regret. "I never meant to betray you. I was hurt and I was angry and I was pissed. But I didn't mean to tell them about you. I thought you were safe back here with Avian when I went with them. I couldn't stay here anymore. I didn't think it would matter if I told them what you were capable of. I wasn't all that sure I'd ever see you again."

I wasn't even breathing as I listened to West apologize. The back of my eyes burned and my throat felt as if it had totally closed off.

"Yell at me," he said, his eyes desperate. "Hit me. Do whatever it takes to make you feel better. I think it will make me feel a bit better if you break a couple bones or knock me unconscious."

From past experience, I knew I was unpredictable when my emotions got away with me around West.

So I did the only smart, reasonable thing I could do in that moment.

I turned and walked away.

"Holy shit," West breathed as I took two steps away from him.

And the way he said it, the way the very air changed around us with his words, made me freeze in place.

I turned to look back at him and found his face stark white. His eyes had reddened and moisture pooled in them.

"What?" I demanded, my tone unsure.

He held a hand over his mouth and squeezed his eyes closed for a moment. A tear streaked down his cheek.

"I have something important to do right now, so if you have something to say, you'd better say it quick."

West finally opened his eyes, wide and disbelieving.

"Now, West!" I demanded, debating just running into the building to complete my task. We could talk later, if we lived through the day.

"You know all those stories I told you? About how we used to play together when we were kids? The notes I left you?" he asked in a shaky voice.

"Is this important *right now*, West?" I said, my tone dripping acid.

He nodded his head.

"Fine, yes."

He paused for a moment. He took a deep, quivering breath. "None of them were true."

"What do you mean?" I asked, my brow furrowing.

"It was your sister, Eve," he said, more tears streaking down his cheeks. His eyes rose to the heavens and he shook his head. "It was your identical twin sister that I did all that stuff with. Not you."

I tried to ask *what?* but the words stuck in my mouth like it had been filled with cotton. My thoughts swirled. I'd seen myself talking to me in those fractured memories and nightmares in Seattle. I'd been crazy, they'd broken my mind. This couldn't be true.

"That tattoo on the back of your head?" he said, his voice shaking nearly beyond control now. "The roman numeral two? You were Eve Two. Your sister was Eve one."

"No," I said, shaking my head, my insides quickly going numb. "No. That can't be…"

West nodded his head. "We hated each other as kids, Eve. Some people just don't get along. You and I, we couldn't stand to be around one another. It…it kind of explains a lot about us now." His brow furrowed, as if reevaluating every moment we had spent together.

"You lied to me," I said, my voice very controlled and very quiet. "Again? About something like *this?*"

Tears started leaking down West's face again and he gave a slight shake of his head. "I thought you were her, Eve one. Because Eve Two was supposed to be *dead*. My father was supposed to dispose of her. Because she had been compromised. Because she killed over fifty people. Because Eve Two did this!" He pulled on the collar of his shirt, exposing the claw marks on his neck.

"That was supposed to be me?" I breathed, not believing a word he said.

West nodded, coming one step closer.

"I never said anything about the twin sister because she was supposed to be dead. You didn't remember anything, and I thought that was for the best. What was the good of bringing up a sister who had tried to kill me and was supposed to be dead? I was going to let the past *stay* dead."

I punched West in the face. Hard enough he collapsed to the ground.

"I can't take any more of your secrets," I said, my voice shaking with rage. "I hate you West Evans, and if we all live through this day, I never want to see you again."

And I left him there on the ground. I slipped inside the building and let the door close behind me.

The interior of the building shifted with lines of black. My hands shook and my stomach rolled in an emotional hurricane.

There was coughing somewhere above me and a quick *shh*. I shut out my personal garbage and took the stairs two at a time.

I was catching a break for the first time in what felt like a very long time. I'd found them in the first building I tried.

Hushed voices came from behind a closed door. Slipping my handgun from my belt, I leaned against the door.

"Do you really think it will work?" a young voice whispered. "Do you really think it can kill them?"

"I don't know baby," a motherly voice said. "We can only hope so."

I pushed the door open, my gun poised ahead of me.

Margaret stood by a large window, overlooking the fight below her.

"I should shoot you right now," I said loudly. Every eye turned on me, including Margaret's There were muffled screams and whimpers.

"Then why don't you?" Margaret asked. There was just the faintest trace of fear in her eyes. But not enough. Not enough to classify her as human in my eyes any longer.

"Because I need to know how far that thing you planted in my head is going to reach."

Margaret didn't answer for a moment and I saw her gaze shift to those around her. I noticed then that they were mostly women, children, and elderly.

"Not here," she said in a hiss and stepped toward me. She held her hands up when I didn't lower the weapon and stopped. Her eyes slipped down to the little girl on the floor just to the side of me who was crying and had her face buried in her mother's shoulder.

"Out in the hall," I said, waving her out with the gun.

The two of us stepped outside the door and I closed it behind us. We walked halfway down the hall for privacy.

"Why?" I asked simply.

"Do you not remember what things were like in Seattle?" Margaret asked with narrowed eyes. "We had to leave or we were all going to get infected. The Underground has been totally compromised. And soon it is going to be the entire world and we will be *eradicated*."

Margaret actually had no idea how true her words were. She had no way of knowing the sweeps the Hunters were conducting.

"Just so you know," I said, my tone turning icy. "You've condemned us all to infection."

"I don't understand your pride with this Pulse thing. You have to use it!"

"We would be happy to," I said, my teeth clenched so tight they might have broken if I were fully human. "If it hadn't been damaged in the earthquake."

Margaret paused, her expression paling. "What earthquake?"

"The one we had just a few days ago. The one that dropped a concrete pillar on the Pulse, making it unusable. And our head scientist, the one who developed it, the only one who can fix it, is sick."

"I didn't know," she said. She was trying to pitch her voice to be non-caring, but she was failing.

"We're all dead now, thanks to you," I said. I grabbed her wrist and started pulling her down the stairs.

Maybe it was shock or guilt or some other unknown conscious that I didn't know she possessed, but Margaret let me drag her out of the building without a fight.

Shots rang out and shouts rose into the air. There were three bodies lying in front of the hospital now. I couldn't look at their faces just then to see if it had been any of ours that had fallen.

West was nowhere to be seen.

"Call your men off," I growled in Margaret's ear. "Or I swear I will kill you right here." I pressed the barrel of my handgun into her ribs.

Margaret shifted uncomfortably, her arm going nowhere under my steel grip. She cleared her throat.

"Cease fire!" Margaret yelled, her voice startlingly loud and filled with authority. "Members of the Underground will assemble. Now!"

Instantly the shots died out and slowly the soldiers, New Eden and foreign alike, gathered before the hospital.

"You have a lot of explaining to do," Royce growled, pointing a finger at Margaret. He approached her, fast. For a moment I was afraid he was going to plow her right over, but he stopped just an inch from her face, his finger pressed to her chest. He was covered in blood and grime.

Avian suddenly came jogging through the crowd, followed by Raj. I resisted the urge to rush at him and pull him into my arms. But now wasn't the time.

240

"I do believe we have some talking to do." She couldn't hide the quake in her voice or the fear in her eyes.

"I should just have Eve shoot you right now," he seethed.

"Trust me," I said, my jaw clenched tight. "It took everything I had in me not to."

"Elijah," Royce barked, turning. Elijah limped forward. There was a shirt tied tightly around his calf, no doubt stopping up a bullet wound. "Watch her people. I swear, if any of them makes a wrong move, shoot them."

Protests were shouted and firearms were raised again.

"You will do as he says!" Margaret bellowed and instantly the contention died. "You will stand down until I come out. You will wait for my word."

Eyes shifted and fingers remained poised on their triggers. But they did lower their weapons. Elijah and his team quickly surrounded the Undergrounders.

"Move," Royce commanded.

Avian stepped forward as if to follow us and Royce immediately threw up a hand. "Now isn't the time to be the protective boyfriend," he said, his voice quiet so the entire crowd wouldn't hear him. "I released you because you're needed out here. This right now is between the three of us."

Avian met my eyes and for a moment there was pain and panic there. I could only nod and try to assure him that somehow, everything was going to be okay.

There was a loud, large crowd just inside the hospital doors. Guards, including Tristan, stood armed and ready with the masses behind them.

"Move!" Royce bellowed as we made our way through the crowd toward the stairs. The tension inside of me built as we ascended.

How much time did we have before we were all dead?

As soon as Royce closed the door to his office he turned and shoved Margaret back into a chair. Her eyes grew wide with fear as she fell back.

Good.

"What have you done?" he growled. He placed his hands on each of the arm rests, his face again coming within an inch of hers.

"If you weren't going to use that Pulse on your own, we thought we'd force you to see reason," she started explaining in a shaky breath. "It was all too easy to plant false information and stage a supposed escape. We knew you'd listen to one of your own soldiers. You would never suspect she was in fact the beacon."

Royce slapped Margaret across the face. The sound was sharp and startling. Margaret jerked to the side, her hair whipping across her face.

"How far is that beacon going to reach?" he demanded.

Margaret faced forward again, her mouth slightly agape, her eyes not quite meeting Royce's. Her hand rose to her cheek gingerly. "We had no certain way to test it. But we estimated it would reach at least five-hundred-miles."

Royce was silent for a moment. I had little doubt he was calculating the size of the cities within that five-hundred-mile radius.

"There is about to be over a million Bane flooding into this city. We were in the middle of an evacuation but there is no way we will get everyone out in time. And we have no way to defend ourselves," Royce said. "What do you have to say about that?"

We heard a shot fired, followed by another.

Royce swore and we both sprinted for the stairwell.

"Do you have any idea how much time we have before they start arriving?" Royce asked as we ran.

I shook my head, tightening my grip on my handgun, wishing I had more firepower. "We were clear for at least seventy five miles. Three hours?"

Royce swore again as we sprinted through the lobby and back out the front doors. There was the faint sound of glass shattering.

The crowd had disbanded again and the fighting resumed.

Elijah lay on the ground, pressing fingers into a bleeding wound in his chest.

Avian had another man pinned beneath him and his fist connected with the man's face. Even West was in the brawl at this point, scuffling in the dirt, his hands wrapped around a soldier's throat.

Down the street another shot was fired.

A woman from the Underground tried rushing the entrance to the hospital. I threw myself at her, knocking her to the ground. We rolled to the ground and she hitched the barrel of her gun up into my stomach.

My breath caught in my throat and I froze on top of her.

"You don't have to do this," I said, my voice breathy. "We are about to be invaded. We don't have time for all this fighting."

"You're one to talk," she spat. "After you just murdered Margaret?"

"What?"

The woman shoved me off of her and pointed somewhere just behind me.

There was broken glass everywhere. And in the middle of it was Margaret.

She was dead. There was no question about it. Her right arm was bent back underneath her at an impossible angle. Her neck was cocked sharply to the left, broken. There were huge chunks of glass embedded into her skin and blood poured from her lifeless body.

"She jumped," I said, my voice horrified and disgusted. I'd heard glass shatter just before Royce and I had gotten back outside.

Royce told her how she'd killed everyone, and she jumped to her death.

"Don't lie to me," the woman said, her voice harsh and emotional. She wedged the barrel of her gun back between my ribs.

"No," I insisted, meeting her brown eyes again. "I promise you, that wasn't us."

The woman's features hardened and she shook her head as she cocked the trigger.

I spun quickly, grabbing her wrist as I did. With a quick flip of my own hand, I pulled the gun from her grasp and completed the spin to turn and point both my own firearm and hers at her chest.

"I will not fire unless I have to," I said quietly. "But right now I am not your enemy. There are about to be hundreds of thousands of Bane flooding this city and I am your only shot at staying alive and human."

And then I knew exactly what I had to do.

Throwing the gun out of her reach, I turned east.

There was a wide open desert out there where no people would get hurt. A wide open desert big enough to hold the enemy that would soon be arriving.

I scanned the fighting crowd for Avian but he was nowhere in sight.

There would be no time for a goodbye.

I dashed around the side of the hospital and dropped down into the garage. I hopped on an oversized ATV. It would get me through the mountains, over the rough terrain, and it would do it quickly.

The engine growled to life and I shot out of the garage.

The crowd parted as I ripped down the street. Members of New Eden shouted after me as I moved. But Royce, Gabriel, and Avian were nowhere in sight.

Spotting Bill, I slowed momentarily. He caught sight of me and I waved him over. He rushed the ATV and hopped on, grabbing onto the cargo rack.

"You're going to head them off, aren't you?" he asked, his eyes serious and dark.

"There's no other way," I said. "We're all dead if I don't do something."

Bill nodded, glancing back at the fighting crowd. They had barely paused when I barreled through them. "Hopefully there are still some of us left to save."

And then West shot through the crowd, stumbling over debris. He stopped next to the ATV, his hands braced on his knees for a moment as he caught his breath.

"I'm sorry I lied, again, Eve," he said, looking up at me with regret on his face. He straightened and pulled something from the cargo pocket of his pants and extended it towards me.

His grandfather's notebook.

"The truth is in there," he said. "You're going to hate me for hiding it, but it's there."

In that moment, there wasn't anything to say. I took the notebook and looked back at the fighting masses, my heart hurting.

"Tell Royce to figure something out," I said. "And tell Addie to be ready with the wireless transmission system. I'll keep them away for as long as I can. But in case I can't keep them all out of the city, continue with the evacuation plan. Head into the water. You'll be safe there. At least for a while."

Bill held my eyes for a long while before he nodded. He placed a hand on the back of my neck and pressed a kiss to my forehead. "Good luck," he said.

"Do me a favor," I said, glancing briefly at West before meeting Bill's eyes again. "Tell Avian that I love him. And that I'm sorry."

"He knows that," Bill said. "But I'll tell him."

I nodded and Bill saluted me.

"I'm sorry," West muttered again as he backed away.

Gripping the handlebars tighter, I revved the engine and took off down the street.

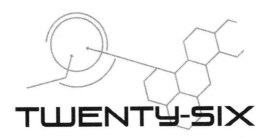

TWENTY-SIX

Even though I could no longer feel that connection to the Bane, I pushed my thoughts out to them. I pictured the desert I had never actually seen. I commanded them to go there and to wait for me.

I was just over an hour outside of New Eden, and had just left a canyon when my ATV sputtered and died. I looked down to see the gas gauge dropping below the red line. Leaving it on the side of the road, I walked.

The land opened up before me, revealing dry desert. There were a few towns hugging the mountains, but after that, nothing but dry open desert.

I know you're out there. Come and find me.

The towns fell behind me and soon my boots crunched over rough, cracked ground. The light breeze that brushed past me tasted stale and dry. When I could no longer see buildings and the landscape was nothing but sage brush, I stopped.

A wind picked up, cool and arid, empty and lonely. I turned my eyes to the horizon, blocking out the blinding afternoon sunlight with my hand.

A figure stepped into view and slowly approached. Another was behind him. Followed by another.

They gathered, one by one, ten by ten. They walked slowly and even, in no hurry and perfectly controlled.

Come.

I shifted uncomfortably as they closed in around me from all sides. Their metal parts gleamed in the sun, their eyes reflecting crazy colors in a prism of light.

The first dozen of them stopped just ten feet from where I was. They stood perfectly still and stared at me.

I was queen of the Bane and these were my subjects.

Night fell and the Bane continued to flock around me. They stretched as far as I could see, filling this desert. There were thousands of them. More than ten thousand. And they all just stood there, facing me.

I sat on the ground eventually when my legs started shaking from standing for endless hours. I commanded the Bane to sit as well, uncomfortable having them stand over me when the last five years I had been trained to fire or run whenever one of these things came in sight.

My eyes were heavy, but I didn't dare fall asleep. What if I did and my connection to them was lost and they headed into New Eden? What about those who were still answering the call of the beacon and heading this way but had not arrived at our gathering place?

My eyelids tried to close, but I held them open until they burned, all through the night.

The sun seemed to rise all at once. It was brilliant and beautiful and so cold all at the same time.

I stood, stretching my stiff limbs and looked out over the crowd again.

There had to now be a few hundred thousand Bane surrounding me. All I could see around me was gleaming bodies that shone in the sun.

Something fell out of my pocket and I looked down to see the notebook.

Loose pages had fallen out of it and it lay open, facing the ground.

The truth is in there, West had said. *You're going to hate me for hiding it, but it's there.*

Bending, I carefully picked up the loose pages and the tattered notebook.

It was open to a page I'd read before.

An unexpected side effect of the chip implantation has occurred. I have been aware of the fact that everything project Eve is able to do should be impossible. The strength, speed, increased eyesight and hearing capacities. This has evolved beyond the capability of the military's chip and TorBane.

The two technologies have intertwined with each other I believe. The chip has given the TorBane technology the ability to spread and evolve. After sedation and a full body scan, hints of cybernetic enhancements have been detected throughout Eve's body. It is not just the brain, lungs, and heart that have been altered now. It is the entire body.

Test's I and II yield duplicate results.

I and II.

It had really been there all along.

My eyes jumped to another entry.

As Eve's brain has continued to develop and evolve, adjustments have been required in II.

Another:

They don't want just one test subject. But how can I in good conscious give them more than that?

The Eve project...

She'd been there too, the entire time.

My sister.

My identical twin sister.

I looked at the loose pages I held in my hand. They were frayed and worn. Like they'd been ripped from the notebook in a hurry.

West had wanted to hide something from me.

I unfolded one, tucking the rest of the pages into the notebook.

It's been a month since my last entry. Eve I has already shown improvements. She's been learning a few more words every week. She is interacting a bit more. Just yesterday we introduced her to my 3 year old grandson, West. We took her to his playroom. He tried to engage her in activities, but she seemed hesitant. Though she did watch him for an hour. She observed the things he did, the way he talked to his toys.

I cannot wait to see Eve I's progress. If she is able to fully recover, this opens up a whole new aspect to this technology. I had never even considered the mental side of TorBane before.

And on the back of the page...

Eve I plays with West three days a week now. She is taken to the playroom and she stays there with him as well as his nanny and her nurse for two hours. She is allowing him to talk to her, though she still will not respond with more than a word or two. But she does try to play with the toys.

It's been eight months since Eve I was given the technology. I don't know if it is because it was given for a neurological condition, but it still seems to work more slowly than I would have hoped. We may try to speed things up with the next generation of testing. We should have it ready in about a year's time.

My hands shook as I read about my sister.

I pulled out another page, dated more than two years prior, and read.

While I has started to stabilize, II continues to languish. The department is fighting against it, saying that the technology is not ready to be tested on a human subject, I feel that I cannot simply let this infant die without trying. It could, and I believe will, save her.

We had been given TorBane for completely different reasons. Mine were physical. Hers were mental.

The truth had been so close to the surface for so long.

I thought about the past, how West had always worded things so carefully when we first met. And the brief look between West and Dr. Beeson when we had first gotten to the hospital. A secret had passed between them then. This secret.

Dr. Beeson.

He wasn't innocent in this either. He knew about my sister as well. He had taken care of us for years! And he never said a word either.

West must have talked him into keeping things quiet.

...let the past stay dead...

Movement across the masses drew my attention from the pages.

One of the Bane was moving closer, working its way through the crowd. As if it had a purpose in reaching me. The others surrounding parted to let it through, but their attention never wavered from me.

I took a step back, stuffing the notebook and pages into my pocket, suddenly unsure of my abilities, but there was nowhere to turn. I was completely surrounded. And there was no one here to save me.

The masses continued to part and I saw a gleaming figure coming through the crowd.

Everything inside of me froze when the Evolved figure finally stepped through the bodies.

"Hello, Eve."

My voice caught in my throat. The Bane no longer spoke and this figure before me was nothing but machinery from the neck down.

But his head was covered in some kind of helmet and the skin of his face was mostly intact. His eyes were human white and West-like brown.

"Dr. Evans?"

He nodded, his eyes bright.

"You're supposed to be dead," I said, my voice barely a whisper.

"And so are you," he replied.

I shook my head, questioning everything I was seeing and hearing. Maybe I was really lying unconscious on the desert floor from dehydration or something. "I don't know what is real any more. I don't even know who I am. My entire life has been a lie."

"I can tell you exactly who you are," he said, his eyes softening. "I can tell you exactly who your sister was."

A lump formed in the back of my throat. I tried to clear it, but it refused to move. "It's true. I really did have a sister."

Dr. Evans nodded. "An identical twin sister. The only way we could tell you apart was your personalities and the tattoos on the backs of your heads."

I lifted a hand to my scalp, running my fingers over the place where I knew my II was.

"Then how can you tell which one I am?" I asked, my eyes narrowing at him.

"Because your sister never would have been able to do this," he said, a hint of a smile pulling on the corner of his lips as he turned and waved a hand over the masses around us. He faced me once more. "You are capable of so much more than you know, Eve Two."

I searched inside of me for the sound of my heart beating. For my erratic breath going in and out my lungs.

I was conscious and this was real.

"Can you answer this," I said, holding his unbelievably human gaze. "Why did everyone think Eve Two was dead?"

He hesitated, regret on his face. "Because you did something that wasn't your fault. Something that in the eyes of most everyone at NovaTor, in the eyes of my son, was unforgivable."

"What?" I asked. "What did I do?"

He shook his head, the fire building in his eyes again. "It doesn't really matter. What does matter is that the reason you were able to do it, is the reason you are going to be able to save the world."

I couldn't answer him for a long moment. His words were impossible, unspeakable. Our world was too far gone. There was no saving it when there was only half a percent left to save. There was no saving it when I was surrounded by possibly millions of Bane.

"That's impossible," I practically whispered, shaking my head. "I can't save the world."

"Oh, that is where you are wrong," Dr. Evans said, a full, plotting smile curling on his lips. "Like I said, you are capable of so much more than you realize. And I had already started plans for the device that will clear our planet."

And the pieces of a puzzle I hadn't even realized where there suddenly fell into place.

"The notebook," the words slipped over my lips. My hand shifted to my pocket.

Dr. Evans nodded his head. "So you've seen the plans."

I reached into my pocket, and slowly, never breaking his gaze, pulled it from my pocket. "West had it. That's how I learned what I really was. We thought the plans were for an electromagnetic pulse."

Dr. Evans broke out in a laugh and clapped his cybernetic hands together. "Brilliant. Just brilliant. Isn't it fascinating how fate works?"

"You're a scientist," I said, holding the notebook tight to my chest, feeling suddenly protective of it. "You aren't supposed to believe in fate."

"Trust me, my dear girl," he said, a gleam in his eye. "In a world where you and I exist, one can't not believe in fate."

"The plans, the drawings," I breathed. "They're not just for your average Pulse, are they?"

"The plans are for something so much bigger," he said, his voice rising in excitement. "And you are the key to making it work."

Something rose up inside of me. Something bigger than me, something that was more hopeful and daring than I. Something that met the sky and the earth and the water. Something that dared to dream of a normal life.

"How?" I asked.

"Are you ready?" Dr. Evans asked. "Are you ready to save this planet, Eve Two?"

"I am."

END OF BOOK TWO

DON'T MISS BOOK THREE

THE EVE

COMING JANUARY 2014

ACKNOWLEDGMENTS

You all have no idea how scary this was to write this book. Committing to writing a trilogy takes guts in a way you can't understand unless you've been there. But it was my readers who gave me the courage. This book never would have been written if you all hadn't demanded it. And I am so glad that you did. So first and foremost, thank you to all of you readers.

Thank you to Jenni Merritt, as always for cheering me along and helping me to plow through messy sentences and scenes. Thank you to Dad, Tim, and Steven for reading this in its early stages and helping me to make it into something people could read.

Thank you to my husband and children who put up with my crazy writing habits. And thank you Heavenly Father, as usual, for giving me the love of writing and everything else.

KEARY TAYLOR grew up along the foothills of the Rocky Mountains where she started creating imaginary worlds and daring characters who always fell in love. She now resides on a tiny island in the Pacific Northwest with her husband and their two young children. She continues to have an overactive imagination that frequently keeps her up at night.

Please visit KearyTaylor.com to learn more about her and her writing process.

Made in the USA
Lexington, KY
16 August 2014